TRAPDOOR TO TREACHERY

KIERAN FANNING

CODE 1 CRACKERS

This puzzle book belongs to

____

MENTOR BOOKS

First Published 2000
by
MENTOR BOOKS
43 Furze Road,
Sandyford Industrial Estate,
Dublin 18.
Tel. (01) 295 2112/3 Fax. (01) 295 2114
e-mail: admin@mentorbooks.ie

ISBN: 1-84210-023-8

The Author

Originally from Stratford-on-Slaney, Co. Wicklow, Kieran Fanning now lives and works as a primary school teacher in Dublin.

Illustrations by Kieran Fanning
Design and layout by Kathryn McKinney
Cover by Jimmy Lawlor

Printed in Ireland by ColourBooks
1 3 5 7 9 10 8 6 4 2

Important Notice – Please read carefully!

This is not an ordinary book. You do not read straight through from beginning to end. Sam and Lisa need your help to solve puzzles and problems that occur in the story. The answer to a problem will be the next page of the story to turn to. Sometimes you will have to turn to a **page number** but sometimes you will have to follow a **symbol**. These are the little pictures at the top left hand corner of every lefthand page. All symbols and their page numbers are listed below.

You must solve the puzzles and problems correctly to find out the next page to turn to. If you are correct you will see the answer in bold print at the top of the page. If you are wrong you should go back and try again. If you get really stuck on any problem there is an answers page at the back of the book.

It might help to write down the page you are working on each time. So if you get the answer wrong you can go back and try again.

Good Luck!

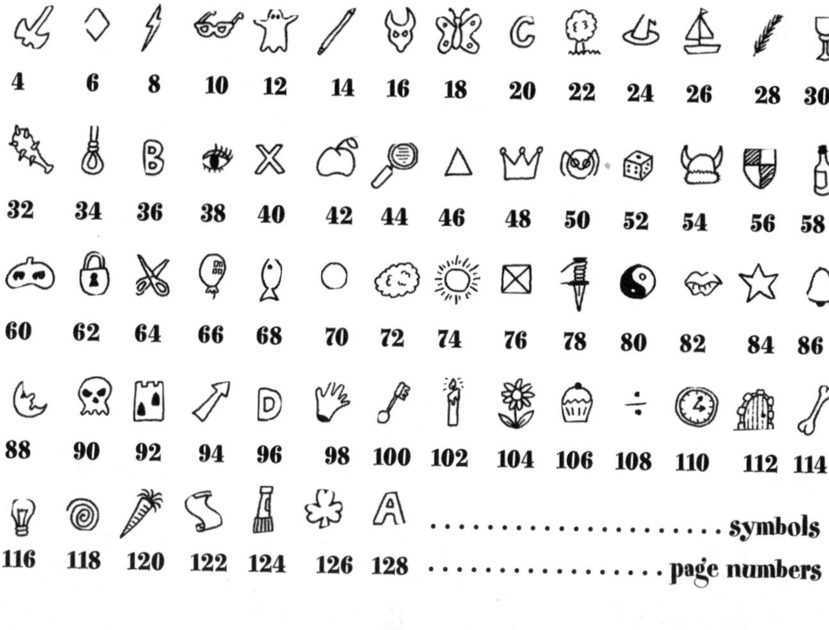

Lowtown was a small quiet place. Sam and Lisa lived there. They were best friends and because neither of them had any brothers or sisters they spent most of their free time together. It was the summer holidays and they were out in Sam's back garden.

They were bored.

'Let's play detectives,' suggested Sam. 'We'll pretend that old Mr Simpson's cat has gone missing and the only thing found on the crime scene was a pair of size nine footprints.'

'I'm sick of pretending,' replied Lisa, with a long face. 'I wish we could investigate something real.'

As if in reply to this request, a voice yelled from the kitchen, 'Sam! Lisa! Come here!'

It was Sam's mother. The children raced into the kitchen. Sam's mother was standing there reading a newspaper.

'It seems that there have been a number of mysterious robberies on Oak Street,' she said. 'That's where Aunt Jane lives.'

'Can I see the paper?' asked Sam.

'Sure,' replied his mother, handing the newspaper to him, 'but don't mess it up or your father will kill you.'

Sam began to flick through the paper at lightning speed looking for the article in question.

'Here it is!' said Sam.

'What does it say?' asked Lisa.

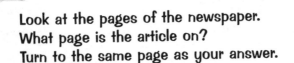

Look at the pages of the newspaper.
What page is the article on?
Turn to the same page as your answer.

Tweetment for sick parrot
Cure for smelly feet
MAN BITES DOG
16
Cheesenham's first win of the season
Fish in wrong plaice at right time
Paper shop blows away!
30

Waterproof Tea-bags?
Mr Bucklewock's at it again
LEOPARD SPOTTED!
20
Another crate of bubblegum found!
Young chimney caught smoking
32

Elephant's trunk lost at airport
Thief used underpants as disguise
38
Mystery thefts shock residents
Teacher flattened by SKATEBOARDER
64

6

Six bottles of 'Reeb' is the correct answer.

'Six,' said Sam as he emptied out the mushrooms and put six bottles of 'Reeb' into the blind elf's bag.

'Those are quality mushrooms,' said the elf. 'I picked them myself in the Crystal Cave just north of the Maze of Mixed-up Messages. Sometimes I think that I'm lucky to be blind. I seem to be the only elf around here that has any free time to pick mushrooms. You see, blind elves aren't much use to 'Mr Greasy Fingers' and so I'm left to my own devices. Thanks again!'

Picking up its bag and tapping its stick on the floor, the elf made its way out the door.

The bell tinkled as the door closed.

'Is there somebody out there?' shouted a voice from the room at the back of the shop.

'Let's go!' whispered Sam.

Swiftly the children slipped back out of the shop without being seen.

Turn back to page 30.

Eight gold coins is the correct answer.

The sound of the gold coins dropping into the wooden bowl amused the gobbledegook. It stood to one side, allowing the children to cross the bridge. Looking behind them, they saw the two gobbledegooks laughing and dividing the gold.

'Well, it wasn't our money anyway!' said Sam, shrugging his shoulders. 'And I only gave them the quarters. Little do they know that all the bigger coins are still in my bag!'

'Nice one!' laughed Lisa, patting Sam on the back.

There was nothing on the other side of the river except a large hole in the ground. The hole led down to another floor.

'It's too far to jump,' said Sam, looking down into the hole. Lisa took the rope out of the rucksack and looped it around the bridge. Then she threw the two ends down the hole.

'Now we can retrieve the rope again when we're at the bottom,' she said to Sam.

'Good thinking,' was his reply.

Using the two pieces of rope, they climbed down through the hole. When they reached the bottom they pulled the rope down after them and replaced it in the rucksack. Looking around Sam and Lisa found themselves in the middle of a large maze with walls made of stone. There were many exits from the maze. Each exit had a number. There was, however, only one way out.

Help Sam and Lisa find their way out.
Which exit is the way out?
Turn to the same page as your answer.

26
32
118
72
16
56
88
106
70
114
42
96
60
78
10
120
24
20
6
50

Card number ten is the correct answer.

'Very good!' said Mammy Long Legs. 'I can see I am going to have to challenge you a bit more.'

She stretched one of her extremely long arms up onto a shelf above the children's heads. Pulling down a jigsaw she handed it to Sam who opened it. It was already made except that one piece was missing. Mammy Long Legs handed Lisa a woollen pouch. The pouch contained many similar, in fact, almost identical, jigsaw pieces.

'Let's see how long it takes you to find the missing piece,' said Mammy Long Legs. 'You have only three minutes.'

Then she picked an egg timer up from the floor and placed it in front of them. The children watched the sand trickle to the bottom of the egg timer. Sam thought it looked wonderful until he felt Lisa punch his arm.

'Stop day dreaming Sam!' she scolded. 'Time is ticking away and we have a job to do!'

'Well there's no need to break my arm!' retorted Sam. 'Anyway this looks simple!'

'Simple,' replied Lisa pointing to the egg timer, 'if there wasn't a time limit!'

A smile crept across Mammy Long Legs' face. 'I love a good argument,' she said.

**Each jigsaw piece is numbered.
Which one is the missing piece?
Turn to the same page as the number on that piece.**

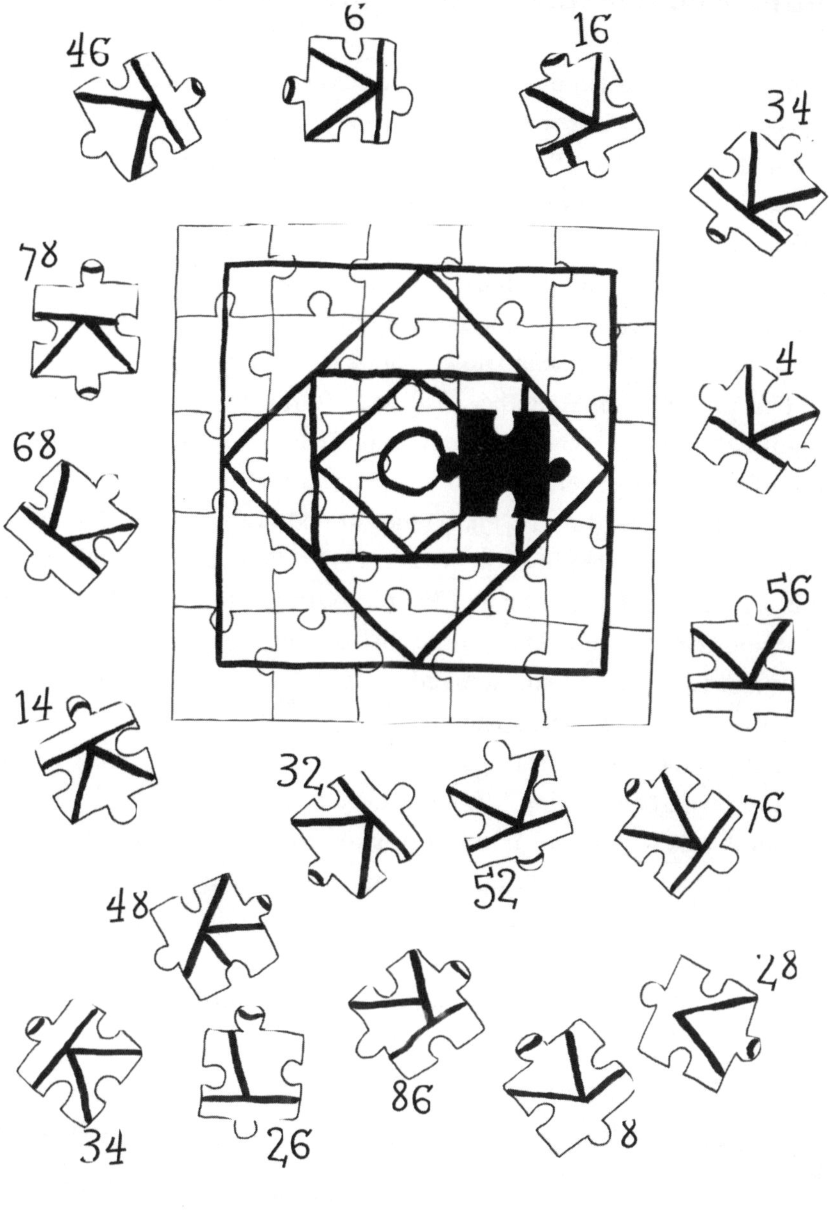
46
6
16
34
78
4
68
56
14
32
52
76
48
28
86
34
26
8

Manhole number twelve is the correct answer.

Sam and Lisa pushed up the manhole cover.

'We're back in Lowtown again!' exclaimed Sam.

'And boy, am I glad!' said Lisa. 'But where's Mr Jones gone?'

Sam pointed across the street. Mr Jones was heading back towards Sunflower Square. To look at him, you would think he was an ordinary man going about his business. You'd never guess he was a master criminal, a professional thief and the holder of many secrets.

'We can't let him escape now!' said Lisa.

The children crossed the road and followed Mr Jones towards Sunflower Square. When he went around the corner, they were able to run without being seen.

Their run slowed to a walk as they rounded the corner. They were now in one of the busiest streets in Lowtown. Cars, buses and motorbikes went zooming by. People pushed and shoved past each other on the footpath. They could just see the top of Mr Jones' head. Sam and Lisa ducked and weaved through the swarm of people but it was no good. They were losing him.

'Keep your eye on him!' panted Sam.

'I'm trying! I'm trying!' shouted Lisa.

But it was hopeless. Mr Jones was too far ahead. If they continued to follow him they would only lose him.

'Which way is he going?' asked Lisa standing on the tip of her toes. 'We may be able to take a shortcut.'

Sam climbed up onto a dustbin. He steadied himself against the wall and frantically scanned the scene in front of him.

Where is he? thought Sam.

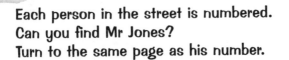

Each person in the street is numbered.
Can you find Mr Jones?
Turn to the same page as his number.

60
44
O'BRIENS
26
62
38
46
12
126
70
SHAM POO
48
8
68
74
110
56
92
76
64
18
16
106
10
94
80
54
30
114
50
52
36
28
96
118
108
6
A Z A
102
88
78

Fourteen is the answer to the skeleton's sum.

'That is correct,' said the skeleton. 'You may now pass through. This has been a secret world for thousands of years. Please keep it that way.'

The skeleton stood to one side, allowing the children to walk past. As they did so, the skeleton offered them a piece of advice.

'Beware of the gobbledegooks,' it said. 'They live near here!'

Accepting, but not understanding, this advice, the children walked through the gateway.

Soon they arrived in a large cavern. What had been making the rushing water sound was now visible. A fast-flowing river surged from a metal grate on one side of the cavern into a metal grate on the other side. The river looked deep and dangerous.

A series of bridges of differing lengths crossed the river. Each bridge had a symbol on it.

'Which bridge shall we cross?' asked Sam.

'The shortest one,' replied Lisa.

Which is the shortest bridge?
Turn to the same page as the symbol on that bridge.

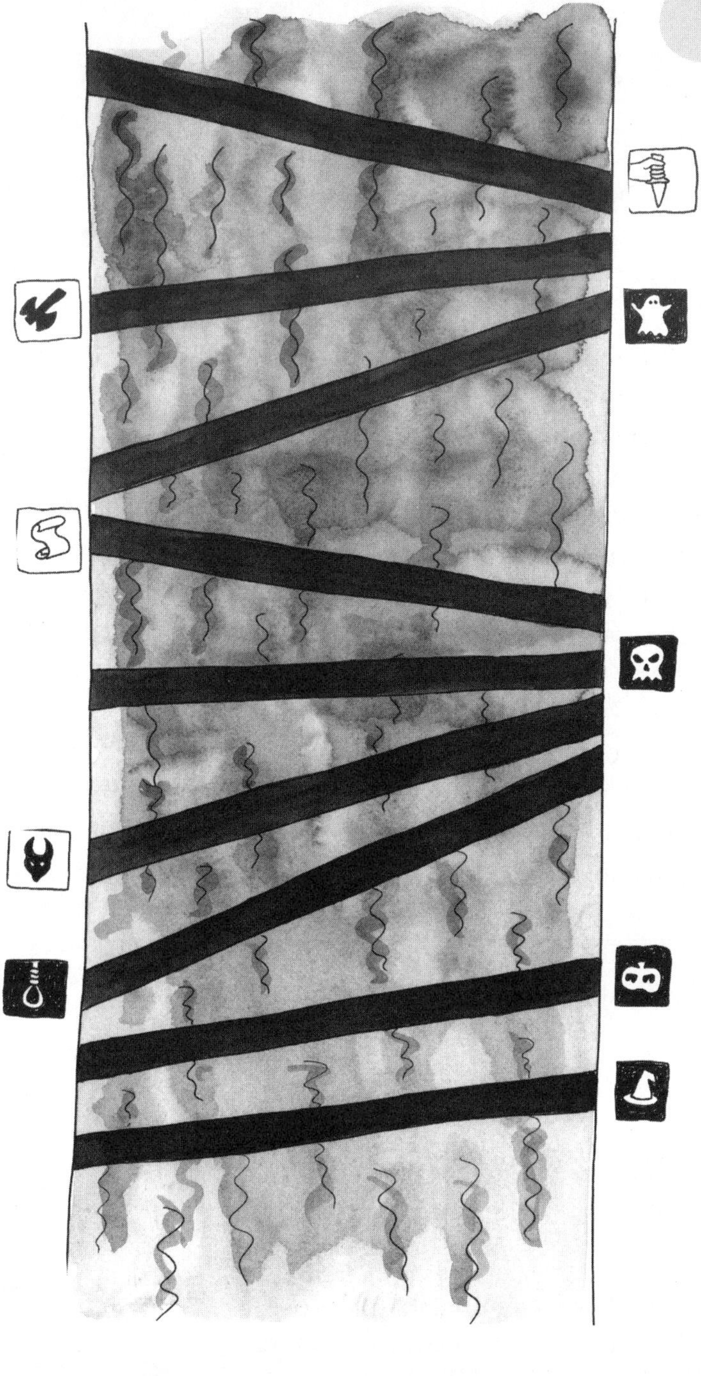

Sixteen coins go into the second bag.

'Thanks,' said the elf, putting the money into two separate bags. 'You think I'm stupid, don't you? Well, maybe I'm not.' The elf picked up the two leather bags, turned and started running away down the tunnel. As it ran, it shouted at the top of its voice, 'Intruders! Help! Help! Intruders!'

The elf disappeared but now Sam and Lisa could hear other voices and the sound of many footsteps approaching.

'Let's get out of here!' urged Sam.

The children began to run back the way they had come. Looking over their shoulders, they could see that they were being followed by a group of elf-warriors. The elves looked angry and carried shields, axes, spears, maces and other dangerous looking weapons. This made Sam and Lisa run even faster, for although the children were bigger than the elves, they were defenceless against such numbers and such weapons.

'Up the ladder!' shouted Lisa.

Like monkeys they climbed the ladder. By the time they were halfway up, the elf-warriors had reached the bottom, but none of them tried to climb up. Instead, they shouted and waved their fists and weapons in the air. Lisa pushed up the wooden trapdoor and disappeared into the ceiling. Sam followed but still the elves remained on the ground. Sam closed the trapdoor behind him.

Find the symbol in the picture.
Turn to that page with that symbol.

Eighteen things is the correct answer.

'Right,' said Sam, 'you take the rucksack. I'll go get the bikes ready.'

He flung the bag at Lisa and galloped down the stairs.

'Where are your manners?' Lisa shouted after him.

She hated when Sam was bossy. He was always bossy when he got excited. Eager not to delay things, Lisa grabbed the bag and raced after him. In her hurry, she forgot to fasten the bag, resulting in all the equipment falling out as she descended the stairs.

'Great! Just great!' she sighed to herself.

She hoped that nothing was broken. Quickly she gathered the things up and put them back in the bag, but something was missing . . .

Can you help Lisa?
What is missing from the contents?
(You may need to go back to page 64.)
Turn to the page with the same symbol.

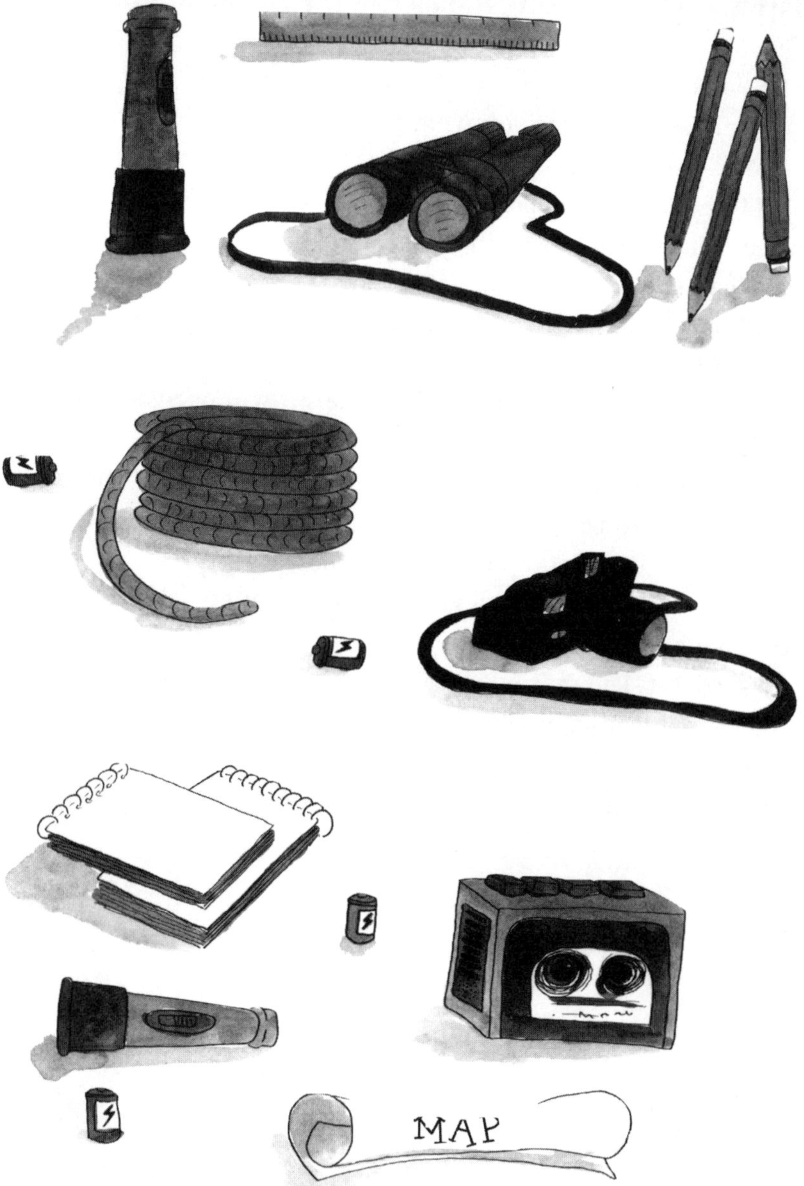
MAP

Twenty is the missing number in the combination.

The safe clicked open.

'There's nothing inside!' whimpered Lisa.

'Wait a minute,' said Sam.

He reached inside and pulled out a piece of paper. It was yellow in places. The edges were torn and wrinkled.

'What is it?' asked Lisa.

'It's a code of some sort,' decided Sam. 'But that's not going to open the door!'

'Maybe not,' smiled Lisa, 'but perhaps it will open one of the other two safes.'

Sure enough, there were symbols above the locks of the other two safes that were the same as the symbols on the paper. Each symbol corresponded to a letter of the alphabet.

'Let's try this one,' suggested Sam pointing to one of the two remaining safes.

'If we translate the code into ordinary letters,' said Lisa, 'it may tell us the combination to open the lock.'

She took out a notebook and pen and began to write out the message, symbol by symbol.

Can you work out the combination for the lock?
Turn to the same page as your answer.

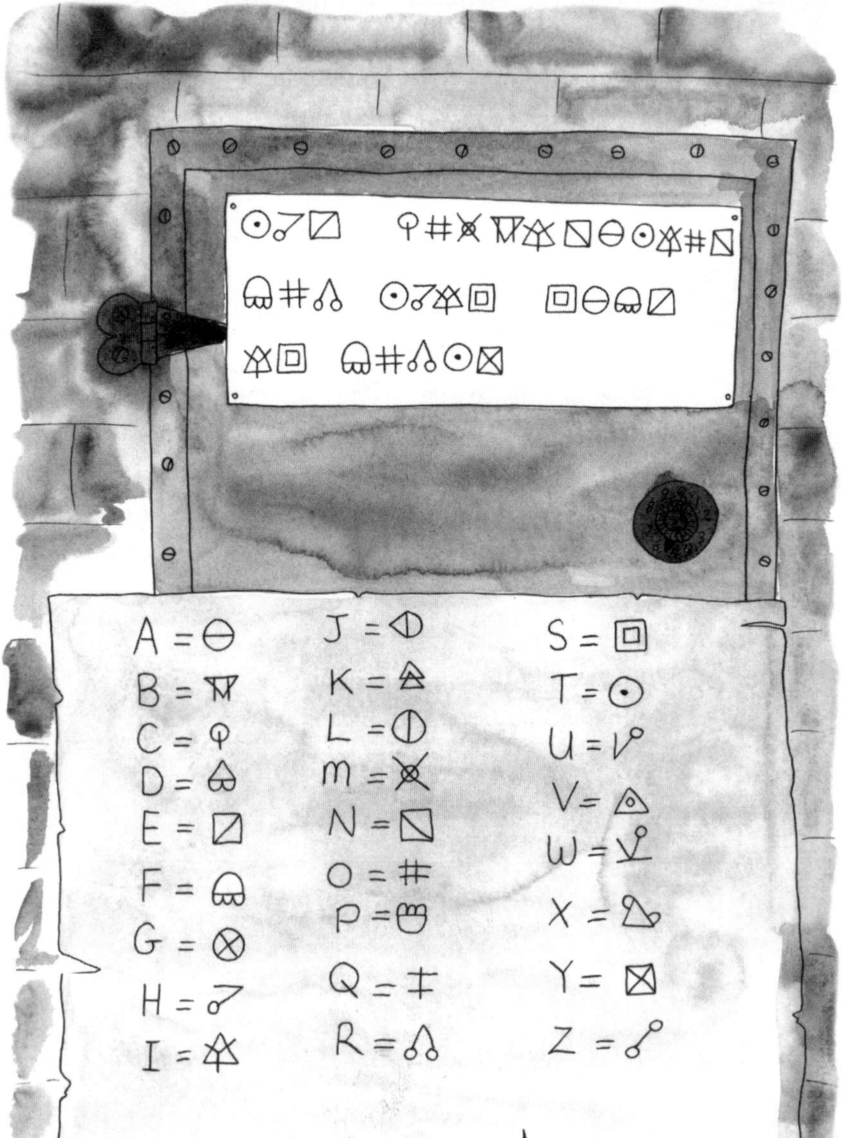
A =
B =
C =
D =
E =
F =
G =
H =
I =
J =
K =
L =
M =
N =
O =
P =
Q =
R =
S =
T =
U =
V =
W =
X =
Y =
Z =

The correct value of the coins is twenty-two.

The children gathered the coins back into the bag.

'What should we do with them?' asked Sam.

'Well they don't belong to us,' replied Lisa, 'so maybe we shouldn't do anything with them.'

'But they're probably stolen property,' said Sam.

He was afraid Lisa would make him leave them behind.

'Yes you're right!' said Lisa. 'We should probably take them back to the police.'

Sam smiled. They put the bag of gold coins into the rucksack and, standing up, suddenly remembered the locked door. They were no longer smiling.

'A million gold coins wouldn't open that door,' sighed Lisa.

'Let's hope that there's a key in this safe,' said Sam pointing to the last safe.

'If not,' he said, 'we're in deep, deep trouble!'

The combination for the third safe was also in code. Sam looked at the sheet of symbols and began decoding the message.

What is the combination of the safe?
Turn to the same page as your answer.

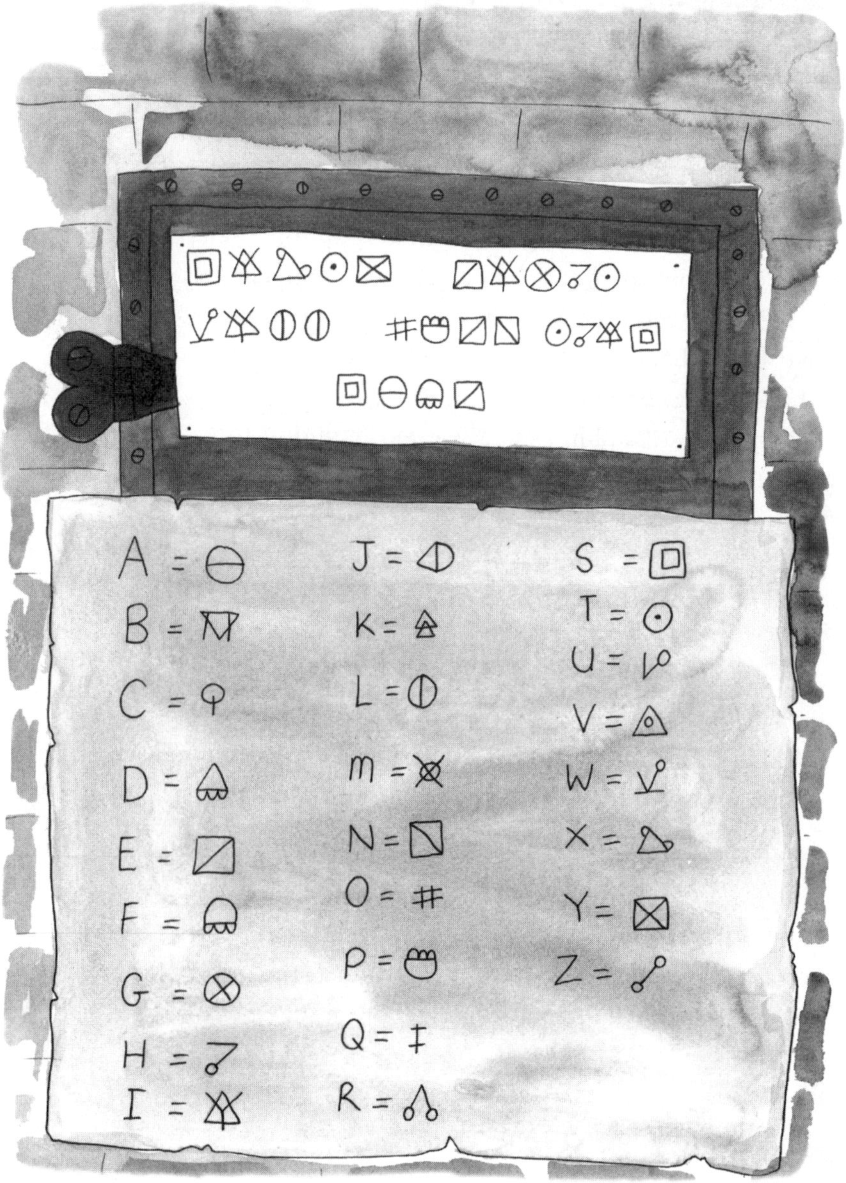
A =
B =
C =
D =
E =
F =
G =
H =
I =
J =
K =
L =
M =
N =
O =
P =
Q =
R =
S =
T =
U =
V =
W =
X =
Y =
Z =

Mr Thompson, 24 Willow Drive.

Hopping on their bikes Sam and Lisa cycled to Willow Drive. Mr Thompson lived in a massive house. It was white with dark drainpipes. A small but neat garden lay in front of the house and a narrow gate led around to the back. Lisa took out the camera and took some photos of the house. Through the windows she got some snaps of the rooms while Sam looked over the side gate into the back garden.

'This guy certainly is rich. He has a swimming pool and a speed boat! Let's check it out!' he suggested.

Lisa shook her head.

'Maybe we shouldn't,' she warned, pointing to a sign in the front garden.

BEWARE OF DOG!
TRESPASSERS WILL BE PROSECUTED
OR
EATEN ALIVE!

'I don't see any guard dog,' said Sam looking around.

'I do!' giggled Lisa. 'Except that it looks more like a cat than a dog!'

Can you see the guard dog in the picture?
Turn back to page 34.

BEWARE OF DOG
Trespassers will
be prosecuted or
eaten alive!

Bus stop number twenty-six is the correct answer.

The children followed Mr Jones to an old, rundown factory. The factory once made gas cylinders but had closed down over twenty years ago. It was guarded by a high rusty fence. Sam and Lisa watched Mr Jones crawl through a hole in the fence and cross an empty yard. They could not follow for fear of being seen. Taking out his binoculars Sam watched Mr Jones walk up to a small shed beside the main factory building. Mr Jones looked all around before entering the shed.

'What a strange place to go!' said Sam

Crouched low to the ground, Sam and Lisa sneaked through the fence and across the yard to the door of the small shed. They listened at the door and heard a clicking noise, a bang and then silence. Sam turned the handle of the door. It creaked as he pushed it. He peeped his head into the shed. There was nobody inside. It was as if Mr Jones had disappeared into thin air.

The shed was full of junk. Everything from pipes to paint, toys to tools, and chains to cogs lay scattered all over the floors, on the shelves and in boxes. A dirty rug covered the floor. Lisa noticed a small lump underneath it. Lifting the rug, they discovered the lump to be a lock.

'That's where he went!' cried Sam.

'Now how can we open this lock?' wondered Lisa.

'There has to be a key around here somewhere,' said Sam. 'There always is in the movies!'

Can you find a key in the shed?
On the key is a number.
Turn to the same page as that number.

GLUE
82
INSTRUCTION
PAINT

House number twenty-eight is the correct answer.

When they arrived at Aunt Jane's, they learned that she had indeed been robbed. She invited the children in for tea and biscuits. The biscuits were so stale that they had to be dipped in the tea before they were edible. Aunt Jane began to tell her story.

'It happened two nights ago,' she said. 'I had put the cats out, closed the windows and locked all the doors. It was only the next morning that I discovered that I had been robbed. The strange thing was that all the doors and windows were exactly as I had left them, closed and locked.'

'What was taken?' asked the inquisitive Lisa.

'My precious lamp was taken,' answered Aunt Jane. 'You know the one, Sam, given to me by your Uncle Hubert on my wedding day.'

Sam pretended he knew and nodded his head.

'It had a square base,' continued Aunt Jane, 'and a striped lampshade and was dotted with circular, triangular and square stones.'

Sam nodded again but was more interested in something else.

'How much money was taken?' he asked.

'I'm not exactly sure,' replied Aunt Jane pulling down a glass jar from a shelf. 'All I know is that I had eighty-eight pounds and now all I have are these few pound coins.'

She emptied the coins onto the table.

How much money was stolen from Aunt Jane?
Turn to the same page as your answer.

Thirty seconds is the correct answer.

Lisa turned to Sam.

'When this guard leaves his post, we have thirty seconds to get from here into the elf village,' she said.

No problem!' replied Sam.

They got ready to run. As soon as the elf-guard left the gate, Sam and Lisa raced across the wide empty space of the cavern and in through the gate of the elf village. No sooner were they in when they saw the next elf-guard approaching. They hid behind a wooden crate. Sam scanned the place with his binoculars. The village consisted of many buildings, most of which seemed to be dwelling houses, but a tavern, a shop, a furnace and a store room could also be seen. Elves walked through the streets minding their own business. It was going to be difficult for the children to explore.

'We've got to be careful,' whispered Lisa. 'Keep away from the main streets, keep low to the ground and if we're spotted, run. If at any time we get split up, return to this spot.'

'Right,' said Sam. 'Now where will we investigate first?'

Investigate four of the buildings in the village by turning to the same page as the number on them.
For example, to investigate the tavern turn to page 114.
When you have investigated all four buildings turn to page 78.

SHOP 88
STORE ROOM
116
RN -114
"ELF" TAVERN
108 - FURNACE

Jigsaw piece number thirty-two is the correct answer.

'Very quick!' said Mammy Long Legs as Lisa handed her the correct piece. 'Now for your final test. And I hope the most difficult. Let's see how long it takes you to find my matching shoe.'

She stuck her foot out to show the children her shoe.

'Check that chest in the corner,' she instructed.

In the corner was a large sea-chest. It was like a pirate's treasure chest made of dark wood and held together by bands of steel.

Lifting up the creaking lid Sam and Lisa found piles of shoes inside. They took all the shoes out and placed them on the floor.

'Your time starts now!' smiled Mammy Long Legs, turning over the egg timer one more time.

'She nearly has as many shoes as you have!' grinned Sam.

'Very funny!' smiled Lisa. 'I'm glad she's not my mammy! I'd need a lot longer than three minutes to find something in my bedroom.'

Like the jigsaw pieces, the shoes were almost identical. There were only slight differences in each one. And what made it even more difficult for the children was the fact that Mammy Long Legs kept pacing up and down the room. She wouldn't stay still long enough for the children to get a good look at her shoe.

'One minute left,' said Mammy Long Legs, pointing to the egg timer.

**Each shoe is numbered.
Which shoe matches Mammy Long Legs' shoe?
Turn to the same page as the number on that shoe.**

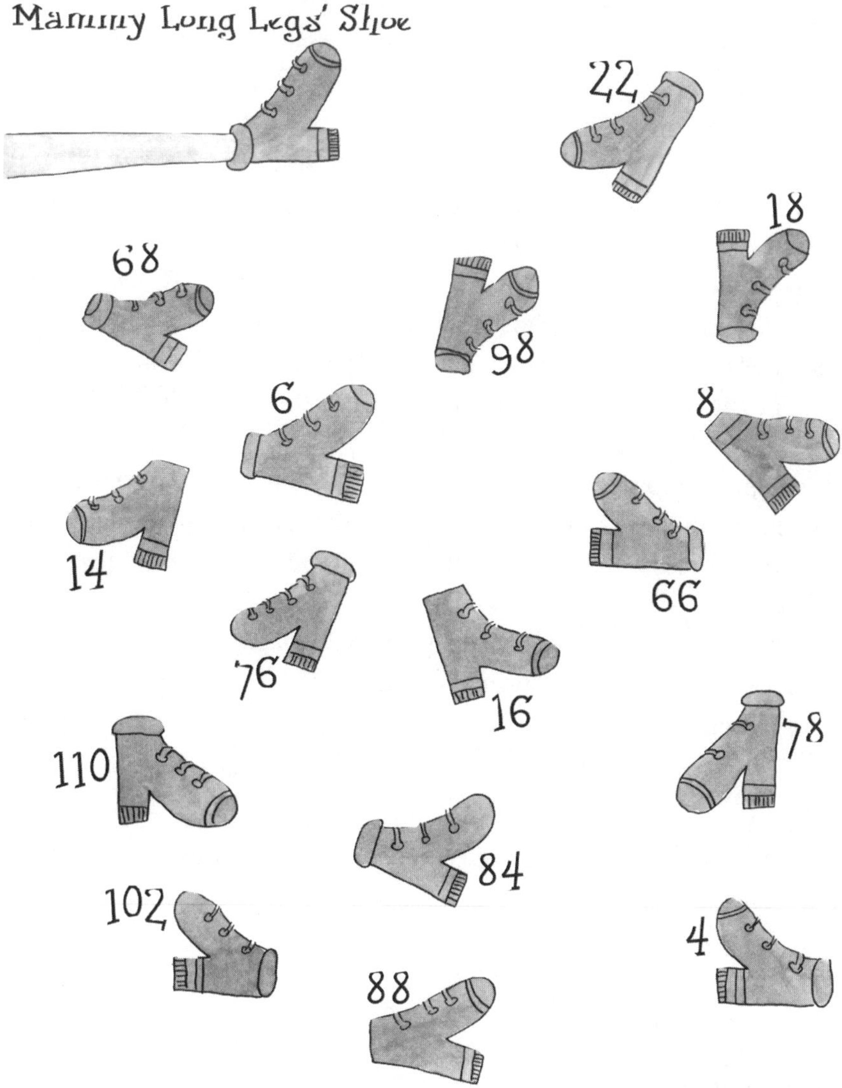
Mammy Long Legs' Shoe
22
18
68
98
6
8
14
66
76
16
78
110
84
102
4
88

Pass number thirty-four is the correct answer.

'Thanks, Lisa,' muttered Sam. 'I hadn't really forgotten, I was just testing to see if you had.'

Yeah, right! thought Lisa desperately trying to hide a smile.

Sam began typing. He hummed a tune to himself.

Don't give up the day job, thought Lisa. She was, however, impressed by Sam's computer skills.

'DOWNLOADING FILES . . . PLEASE WAIT' flashed on the monitor screen. Both children silently focused their attention on the screen. The computer beeped and the required information appeared.

'Got it!' shouted Sam clenching a fist in the air. 'Now let's print it out.'

The printer made a buzzing noise as the printout began to appear.

'This,' said Sam pointing to the emerging paper, 'should tell us the names, addresses and bank balances of the four richest people in Lowtown.'

The printing complete, Lisa examined the page.

'These are our four suspects,' she said.

'Let's check them out!' said Sam already unplugging the computer.

Investigate each of the four suspects by turning to the same page as the number of their house.
For example, to investigate Mr Thompson, turn to page 24.
When you have investigated all four people, turn to page 86.

LOWTOWN'S RICHEST RESIDENTS

Name	Address	Savings
Mr Johnson	• 60 Crown Street	• £230,000
Mr Jones	• 98 Old Street	• £150,000
Mrs Brown	• 122 Spider Street	• £130,000
Mr Thompson	• 24 Willow Drive	• £85,000

Mr Jones took exit number thirty-six.

The stars in Mr Jones' footprints were a giveaway. Sam and Lisa followed his trail through the exit. An iron gate led to steps reaching upwards. They started climbing. All along the steps were junctions with more steps that led upwards or downwards. It was so dark that the children had to feel their way along the walls using their hands. As they climbed higher, it did, however, seem to get brighter or else they were just getting used to seeing in the dark. At first they could only hear footsteps ahead of them but then they caught sight of a man. Mr Jones! The children followed quietly. Black arrows were visible on the steps and it seemed as if Mr Jones was following these.

Soon the steps suddenly came to an end. Mr Jones stopped and pushed at something above his head. Bright light flooded in over him. Sam and Lisa watched him climb out through a manhole. The lid was replaced and once again the children were left in darkness.

'Let's go!' shouted Sam, running up the steps. Coming to the top he stretched his arms up. 'I can't reach,' he cried, looking at the manhole cover above his head.

'Let me up on your shoulders!' urged Lisa.

Swiftly she climbed onto her friend's shoulders and with one almighty heave, she pushed the cover up. The bright light stung her eyes. Lisa scrambled up through the hole. With a jump Sam caught the edge of the hole and climbed out.

Which manhole did Mr Jones and the children climb out of?
Turn to the same page as your answer.

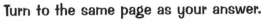

20
90
12
8
54
96

Thirty-eight minutes is the correct answer.

Sam and Lisa arrived at Sunflower Square at 11.58.

'We've two minutes to find Mr Jones,' said Lisa.

As they had suspected it would be, the square was crowded with people. Some people were rushing here and there, others strolled about enjoying the midday sun. A man sat by the fountain reading a newspaper. A lost child cried for his mother. An athlete attempted to jog through the crowds. A couple enjoyed a drink under the shade of a huge umbrella. There were all sorts of people around, from conductors to cowboys and priests to punks. The children looked around frantically. They still hadn't spotted Mr Jones.

'Average height, bald, with glasses,' Lisa reminded herself.

'C'mon,' said Sam, 'there can't be that many people wearing a shirt and tie and carrying a briefcase.'

The children carefully scanned the area but without success. The square was too crowded.

'I can't see anybody fitting that description,' sighed Lisa.

Sam frowned. 'I've just realised,' he said, 'that the note didn't have a day or date on it. It could have been written a week ago!'

He picked up his bike and was getting ready to leave when Lisa grabbed his arm.

'I see him!' she whispered excitedly, pointing into the square.

Each person in the square has a number.
Can you find Mr Jones?
Turn to the same page as his number.

12
96
20
14
4
84
58
100
66
72
40
80
10
70
30
26
34
94
32
76
64
48
18
54
78
82
22
2
62
86
38
88
42
56

The combination for this safe is forty.

The safe clicked open. This time Lisa put her hand in. She pulled out a brown leather bag, opened it and looked in. A golden glow came from the bag. Lisa's eyes lit up.

'What is it? What is it?' begged Sam impatiently.

Lisa knelt down on the ground and emptied out the contents of the bag. Sam couldn't believe his eyes. A pile of gold coins lay before them.

'Wow!' he said picking one up. He put it between his teeth and bit it. 'Pure gold!' he gasped.

Engraved on the coin was the number one. All the coins were different sizes and had different numbers on them. The small ones were only halves and quarters.

'Let's find the value of them all,' Lisa suggested to Sam.

'How do we do that?' he asked.

'Just add them all up. Two halves make a whole and four quarters make a whole,' Lisa replied.

What is the total value of the coins?
Turn to the same page as your answer.

ONE
ONE
THREE
4
FOUR
FIVE
ONE

Photo number forty-two is the correct answer.

'If your Aunt Jane's lamp is in Mr Jones' house then we can be pretty sure that Mr Jones is our thief,' exclaimed Sam.

'Oh, listen to the genius,' mocked Lisa. 'But, yes, you're right.'

'Now how are we going to find this Mr Jones?' asked Sam. 'We know nothing about him other than where he lives.'

'Well then, let that be our starting point,' said Lisa. 'He has to come home sometime.'

The children got their gear and headed back to Mr Jones'. Lisa knocked on the door. No answer.

'Let Operation Jones begin,' whispered Sam, already making his way over the side gate and into the back garden.

Lisa followed reluctantly. The back door was locked but one of the back windows was open. Within seconds, Sam had climbed onto the windowsill and disappeared in through the open window. Lisa was scared to go into the house but even more scared of being left on her own. She quickly followed Sam through the window.

She found him in the sitting room searching through the contents of the rubbish bin.

'Let's just take the lamp and go!' whispered Lisa pointing to the lamp in the corner of the room.

'No,' replied Sam. 'If Mr Jones finds the lamp missing, he'll know somebody's on to him. A good detective doesn't just recover the missing article but solves the mystery as well. We've got to look for some clue to his method of robbery.'

The longer Lisa stayed in the house, the faster and louder her heart beat. Suddenly Sam called her over to the bin.

'Look!' he exclaimed, showing Lisa handfuls of bits of paper. 'It's a note of some sort except that its torn up into many pieces. Let's try and work out what it says.'

Can you work out what the note says.
The note will tell you to follow a symbol.
Turn to the same page as that symbol.

The magnifying glass is the correct answer.

Because Sam's memory was so bad, he had forgotten exactly where Aunt Jane lived. His mother gladly helped out.

'When you arrive between the two car parks, head for the cinema. Take the first left and then the second left. Turn left at the end of that road. Turn left after the traffic lights. Take the footpath from the car park. Take the second left, follow the path and cross the river. Turn right and continue along the river. Cross back over the river on the first, no, the second pedestrian bridge. Turn left, then right after the gym. Take the second right. Aunt Jane lives in the second house on the left,' she said.

'Got that, Lisa?' asked Sam.

'Roger,' replied Lisa.

Helmets were put on, bikes were mounted and the cycle began. Sam, of course, flew off ahead of Lisa. She smiled to herself knowing that he would not go too far on his own. Soon they arrived between the two car parks. Lisa took out the map.

'Now let's see . . . ' she mumbled to herself.

What number house does Aunt Jane live in?
Turn to the same page as your answer.

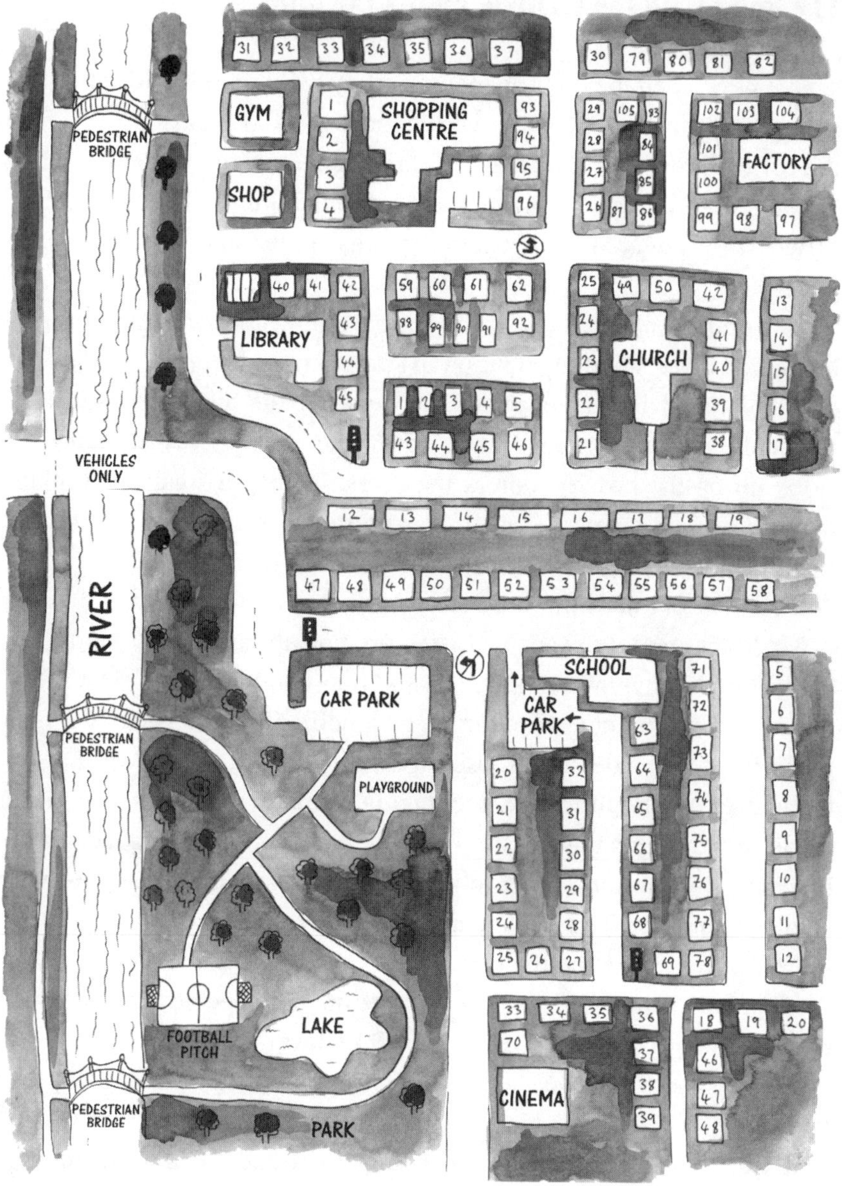
GYM
SHOPPING CENTRE
SHOP
PEDESTRIAN BRIDGE
FACTORY
LIBRARY
CHURCH
VEHICLES ONLY
RIVER
CAR PARK
SCHOOL
CAR PARK
PEDESTRIAN BRIDGE
PLAYGROUND
FOOTBALL PITCH
LAKE
PEDESTRIAN BRIDGE
PARK
CINEMA

The lever with the triangle opens the door.

They knew when the door opened that they had found Mr Jones' office. A large window on one wall overlooked a vast cave and steps led from the office down into the cave. A control panel in front of the window contained a microphone, levers and various buttons. The walls of the office were covered with charts, graphs, notes and other pieces of paper.

Sam and Lisa looked out of the large window. Below them more than a hundred elves stood to attention in straight lines facing a wooden box. None of them moved an inch. There were exits all around the cave. Suddenly, a figure emerged from one of the exits. It was Mr Jones. He stood up on the box to address the elves. He had a small microphone hanging around his neck, which was presumably connected to the four large speakers on the walls of the cave.

Lisa took out her mini tape recorder and pressed 'record'.

Mr Jones started to speak. 'Listen up, you slimebags,' he said. 'Last night the takings were low. That's not good enough! I want an improvement tonight. Our target is Smellington Street so get your green little backsides into those pipes, up out of those toilets and into the homes on Smellington Street taking as many valuables as you can. I want none of this business of bringing back one gold necklace or one bracelet. I want your hands full! Do you understand?' The elves were silent. 'I said: Do You Understand?!' shouted Mr Jones.

'YES, SIR!' shouted the elves.

'Gotcha!' said Lisa, clicking 'stop' on her tape recorder. 'That's enough to put you away, Mister Not-So-Clever Jones!'

'There's more evidence here,' said Sam, pointing to a piece of paper on the wall.

It was a map showing a street of houses and the sewers that ran underneath.

'There's only one house on this street that can be robbed by those elves,' said Sam looking at the map.

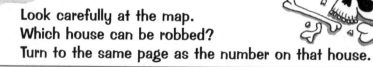

Look carefully at the map.
Which house can be robbed?
Turn to the same page as the number on that house.

Key number forty-eight fits the lock.

The large wooden door opened easily into a long narrow passage. The passage was dark but there was enough light for Sam and Lisa to see where they were going. As they were walking along, the ground beneath their feet felt strange. With every footstep there was a crunching noise. Lisa took out her torch. She screamed when she realised what she was standing on. The floor of the passage was covered with bones. Human bones! The torch light revealed a carpet of human skeletons. They lay twisted and tangled on top of each other. Empty eye-sockets in dusty skulls stared up at them. Mouths with missing teeth gaped as if trying to warn them about the danger ahead.

'Let's go!' whispered a pale-faced Sam, tugging at Lisa's arm.

Carefully they proceeded along the passage. Gradually it got brighter and there were less and less skeletons on the ground until eventually the children stepped over the last pile of bones. The sound of flowing water could be heard in the distance. They could see light at the end of the passage but something was blocking it. A tall figure, dressed in a black cloak, sat on a stool. Although it was facing them, Sam and Lisa couldn't see its face because it was covered with a hood. It was motionless. Cautiously, they approached the figure. It didn't move. They inched closer and closer. They were now within arm's reach of the figure but still it remained lifeless.

Multiply the number of skulls in the picture by fourteen and subtract two.
Turn to the page with that number.

The elf symbol is page fifty.

'Well done, Lisa,' whispered Sam. 'Now I remember. That symbol was on one of the safes and on the sign outside the shop.'

When Lisa had finished drawing the symbol on the slate, the elves seemed surprised but were convinced. They mumbled something and then returned to their game. Whispers circulated the tavern and soon the whole place was under the impression that the children worked for Mr Jones.

'Now that we've been discovered, let's use it to our advantage,' whispered Lisa to Sam.

'What do you mean?' asked Sam.

'I mean let's walk around the tavern and see if we can find out anything,' she said.

'Fine,' agreed Sam, 'but at the first sign of trouble we're out of here, OK?' Lisa nodded.

The children walked in between the tables. Elves turned their heads and squinted suspiciously. They looked nervous when the children approached them. Lisa could make out bits and pieces of a low conversation between three elves sitting at a table.

'Jones . . . slaves . . . life . . . escape . . . the good old days . . . die.'

When she approached them to hear more, they shut up. None of the elves seemed to want to have anything to do with the newcomers.

'Ever get the feeling that you're not wanted?' Sam remarked.

'Yeah. Perhaps we should go,' Lisa replied. 'The longer we stay the more dangerous it's going to get.'

The children left as quietly as they had entered.

Turn back to page 30.

House number fifty-two can be robbed.

Suddenly the children heard a lot of commotion in the cave below. Lisa raced back to the window and looked down. It was chaotic. Elves were running all over the place. They seemed to be disappearing into exits all around the cave. There was no sign of Mr Jones.

'Quick,' shouted Lisa, 'he's getting away.' She ran towards the door. 'Take that map as evidence,' she called back to Sam.

She disappeared down the steps into the large cave where the meeting was being held. Sam tore down the map of street houses and sewers and followed. By the time Sam reached the cave the place was empty except for Lisa and clouds of dust caused by the running elves.

Neither Mr Jones nor any of the elves were to be seen anywhere. There was nothing except footprints, different footprints leading into different exits.

Which exit did Mr Jones take?
Turn to the same page as the number on that exit.

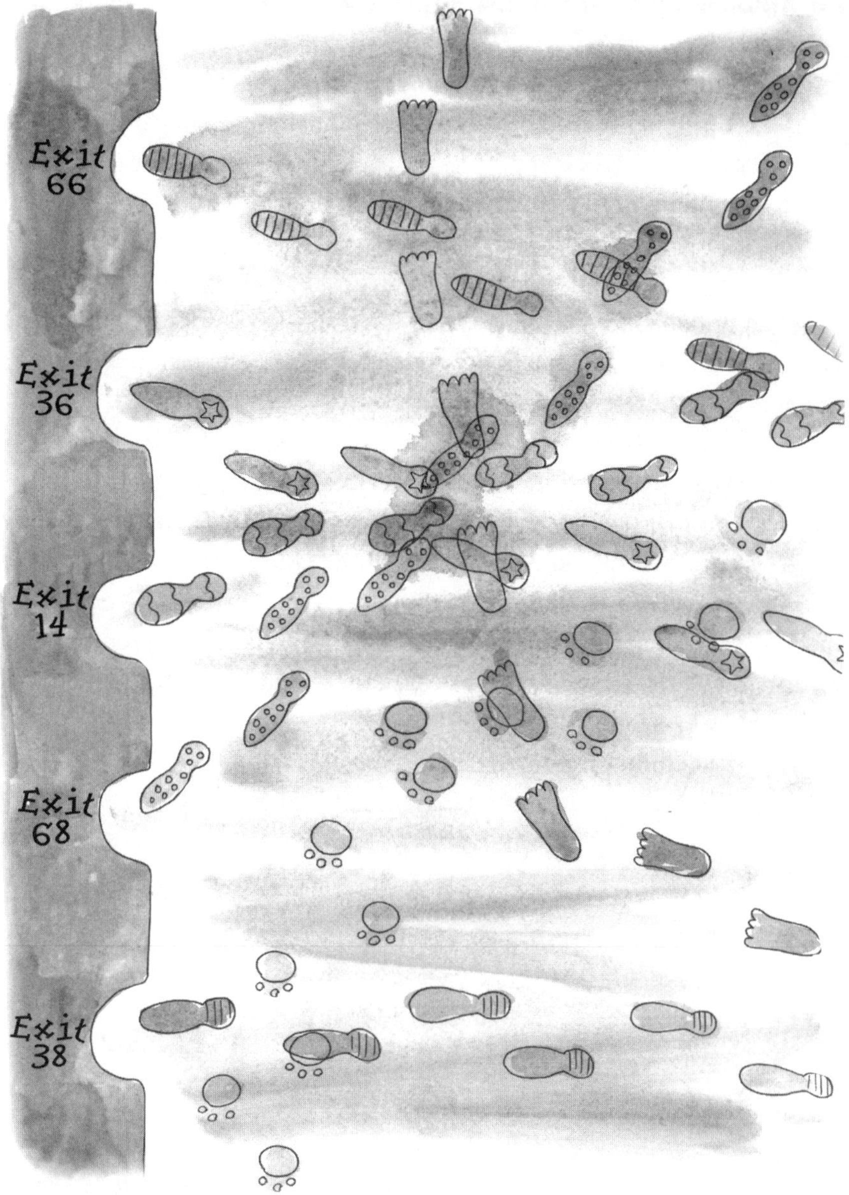
Exit 66
Exit 36
Exit 14
Exit 68
Exit 38

Elf number fifty-four is the correct answer.

Salca left the furnace and continued up the street. He stopped briefly to pick up and examine some food outside a shop. When the shopkeeper emerged he replaced it and kept walking. It was obvious that he was new to the village because he didn't seem to know where he was going. He kept looking around, walking first in one direction, changing his mind and then walking in another direction.

When nobody was looking the children dashed across the street and continued around the back of a small house. They stopped at the corner.

'We're losing him!' said Sam.

They could just about see Salca. He was standing at the side of the street looking at a piece of paper. The children kept their eyes firmly fixed on him. All of a sudden a cart full of crates was pulled onto the street by two elves. As they pulled it up the street everybody got out of their way. Passing between Salca and the children, the cart temporarily obstructed their view of the elf. When it had gone by, Salca was nowhere to be seen.

'We've lost him,' muttered Sam.

'Forget it,' said Lisa. 'Let's keep looking around.'

Turn back to page 30.

108 - FURNACE

Exit number fifty-six is the way out of the maze.

As the children negotiated their way out of the maze, they noticed footprints on the ground. A man's footprints! In the heel of each footprint was a star shape.

'They must be Mr Jones' footprints,' said Sam.

They followed the footprints out of the maze and into a narrow passage. They passed by a ladder leading up to a wooden trapdoor in the ceiling. The footprints, however, led them to a sharp bend in the passage. The sound of an angry voice drifted towards them.

'Listen,' said the voice, 'if you can't count the money, then what good are you to me? You either do what I ask you to do or else . . . Let's just say "Or else"!'

Sam peeped around the corner just in time to see Mr Jones walking further along the passageway.

Sitting on the ground was a strong-looking elf-like creature. It was green with large ears. Gold coins were in piles on the floor all around the elf. All of a sudden it burst into tears. Lisa decided to investigate.

'What's wrong?' she asked.

The elf jumped to its feet.

'Intruders!' it squeaked. 'You're not supposed to be here!'

'We know that,' said Lisa, 'but maybe we can help you.'

The elf squinted its eyes with suspicion. It looked over its shoulder and then said, 'OK! My problem is that I have to divide forty-eight coins into two bags with the first bag having twice as much as the second. No matter how many times I try, I still can't do it.'

'Simple!' said Lisa.

How many coins should go into the <u>second</u> bag?
Turn to the same page as your answer.

The bottle is the correct answer to the riddle.

SAM
A
N
D
L
I
S
A WERE GETTING
V
E
R
Y
TIRED OF M
I
X
E
D
UP
MESSAGES BUT STILL T
H
E
Y HAD TO P
R
E
S
S
O
N

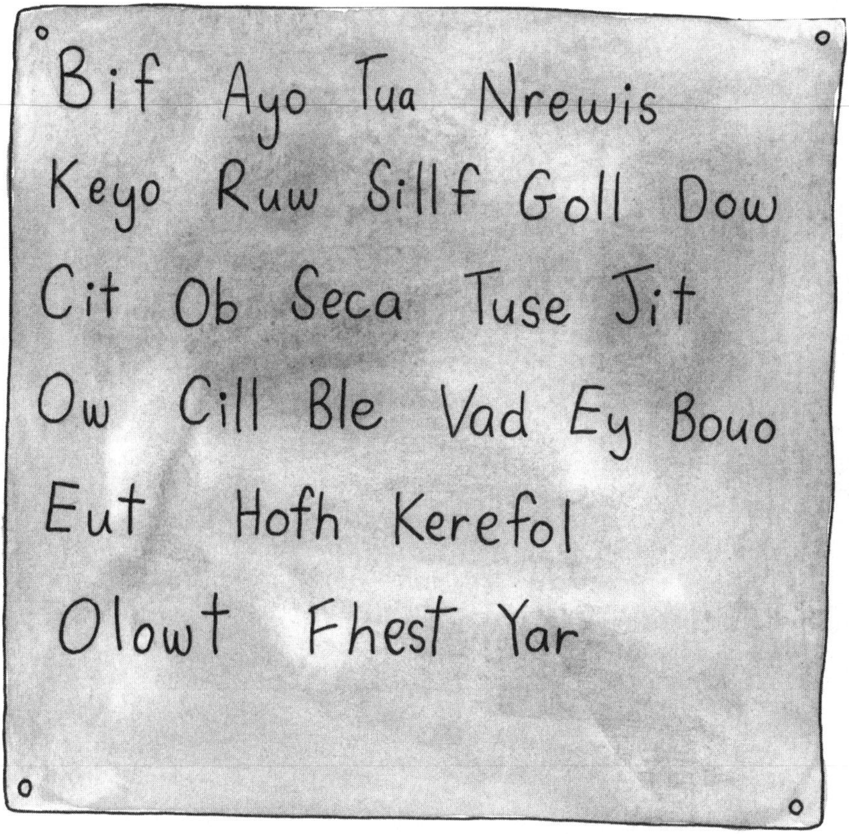
Bif Ayo Tua Nrewis
Keyo Ruw Sillf Goll Dow
Cit Ob Seca Tuse Jit
Ow Cill Ble Vad Ey Bouo
Eut Hofh Kerefol
Olowt Fhest Yar

Mr Johnson, 60 Crown Street.

When the children arrived at Mr Johnson's house, Sam knocked on the door. A tall man with long black hair opened it. He was dressed in a grey suit and white shirt with pointed collars and his eyes were hidden by a pair of sunglasses. Seventies dude! thought Sam.

'Are you Mr Johnson?' asked Sam, a little nervously.

'Yes,' replied the man.

'I'm a reporter for the school newspaper,' said Sam, taking out his notepad and pencil, 'and we're doing an article on successful business people in the area. Could you tell us a bit about yourself?'

While Sam kept Mr Johnson talking, Lisa went around the side of the house with her camera.

'Well, you've come to the right place,' smiled Mr Johnson. 'I'm probably the richest and most successful person in Lowtown. I have three tennis courts at the back, a sports car and a yacht. The funny thing is that I don't play tennis and I hardly ever get time to go sailing. It's my wife, you see. She likes her status symbols.

'I make my money from buying up houses and then renting them to people. I have nine houses here in Lowtown and another five in the country. I also have a few business interests elsewhere but maybe I shouldn't tell you too much.' Mr Johnson laughed a hearty laugh.

Sam continued writing in his notepad, taking down everything Mr Johnson said.

'Anyway,' continued Mr Johnson, 'I must go because I'm purchasing my twelfth house this afternoon and maybe I will do a bit of sailing now that you've reminded me.'

'Thank you for your help,' said Sam, looking up from his notepad.

Mr Johnson smiled and closed the door. As Sam looked back over his notes, he realised that Mr Johnson had not been truthful about everything.

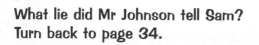

What lie did Mr Johnson tell Sam?
Turn back to page 34.

Sixty-two steps is the correct answer.

Eventually Lisa arrived at the bottom of the steps. They shone their torches around and found that they were standing in a stone room. There was nothing in the room. The children could feel a cold draught blowing across the room yet they could see no doors or windows.

It has to be coming from somewhere, thought Lisa.

The floor was made up of large square stone tiles. Each tile had a letter carved onto it. Lisa tried to make sense of the letters. Her concentration was interrupted by Sam.

'Hey Lisa!' he called, 'Look at this!'

Sam shone his torch onto a rusty sign on the wall. It read:

WHAT YOU ARE LOOKING FOR
IS ON THE FLOOR.

Sam and Lisa looked at each other and then at the floor.

'What can that mean?' asked Sam with a baffled look.

'I don't know,' replied Lisa still examining the floor, 'but we're obviously looking for a word. It's like a giant wordsearch. What you are looking for is on the floor. Now what are we looking for?'

'A way out of here?' suggested Sam.

'Keep looking,' urged Lisa, 'it can't be that difficult!'

What are they looking for?
Turn to the same page as that symbol.

What you are
looking for is
on the floor

Newspaper page sixty-four is the correct answer.

Sam began to read the article.

> MYSTERY THEFTS SHOCK RESIDENTS
> One by one, the residents of Oak Street, Lowtown are becoming victims of a mysterious thief. Valuables and money have been taken from various homes at night in a manner which has left the police dumbfounded. 'The thief or thieves,' explained Sergeant U. Sless, 'have entered locked, alarmed and mostly occupied houses during the night, raided these homes and then left without any noise or clue to their identity.' No forced entry has been visible in any of these houses.
>
> The police continue to search for this mysterious thief.

'Wow!' said Sam looking up from the paper. 'This calls for some detective work. I hope poor Aunt Jane hasn't been robbed.'

The newspaper was flung onto the kitchen table and the children raced up to Sam's bedroom. At last they had something to do.

'Right,' said Sam, 'let's pack our equipment. Oh yeah, Mum says I can use her new computer sometimes for research projects and stuff. You never know, we might need it. The pass number is thirty-four. I want you to remember that because you know what my memory is like.'

'And what if I forget?' replied Lisa.

'If you forget, then we won't be able to use the computer, will we? Muttonhead!' sneered Sam.

Into a rucksack they put two torches, two notepads, three pencils, a ruler, Lisa's camera, a magnifying glass, a tape recorder, a rope, a pair of binoculars, four spare batteries and a map of Lowtown.

How many things did they put into the rucksack?
Turn to the same page as your answer.

FOOTBALL
MAP

Shoe number sixty-six is the correct answer.

'Excellent,' said Mammy Long Legs, who was obviously excited about her newly found shoe. 'You have done well and entertained me amply. Now, how can I help you?'

'We're after a man called Mr Jones,' said Lisa.

'Bald, ugly, with glasses?' asked Mammy Long Legs.

'That's him,' replied Sam.

'Thankfully he leaves me alone,' declared Mammy Long Legs. 'I'm too smart for him. It's those elves I feel sorry for.'

'Do you know where we can find him?' enquired Lisa.

'His hide-out is a long way from here but I can show you a shortcut. If you go through this door behind me, you will come to the Maze of Mixed-Up Messages. Find your way through the maze and you will come to a large cave with many exits.'

Mammy Long Legs took a pot of ink, a feather and a piece of paper from a drawer. She began writing at an amazing speed on the paper. Sam wished he could do his homework that quickly. A few seconds later, she handed them a map of the cave in question, with a set of instructions at the bottom.

'These instructions will tell you which exit to take from the cave. If you follow the correct exit, you will come to the elf village. There you should find your Mr Jones,' said Mammy Long Legs, opening the wooden door behind her.

The children thanked her and walked through the door.

**Find the symbol in the picture.
Turn to the page with that symbol.**

Sixty-eight will open this safe.

'Please let there be a key in this safe!' prayed Lisa.

Sam had his fingers crossed. Lisa pulled open the door of the safe. Inside was a wooden box. She lifted it out and opened it.

'Oh no!' she groaned.

Lisa hadn't found a single key but a box full of them. The keys were brown and rusty and they all looked identical.

'Now all we have to do,' said Sam, 'is to figure out which key opens the door.'

'Easier said than done,' sighed Lisa. 'We could be here all night.'

'Well, it's our only hope,' was Sam's reply as he picked up the first key and went over to try it in the lock.

It wasn't the correct key. Sam put it to one side and tried another. Lisa sat down on the dusty floor and stared up at the ceiling.

'I'm starting to regret wishing for adventure this summer,' she said. 'If adventure means being locked in a dark, dusty room with a bunch of keys that don't work and a bag of gold that's practically useless, I think I'd prefer to be bored any day!'

Sam mumbled to himself. He wouldn't give up. He hadn't tried all the keys yet!

In the circle is a picture of the inside of the lock.
See which key fits the lock.
Turn to the same page as the number on the correct key.

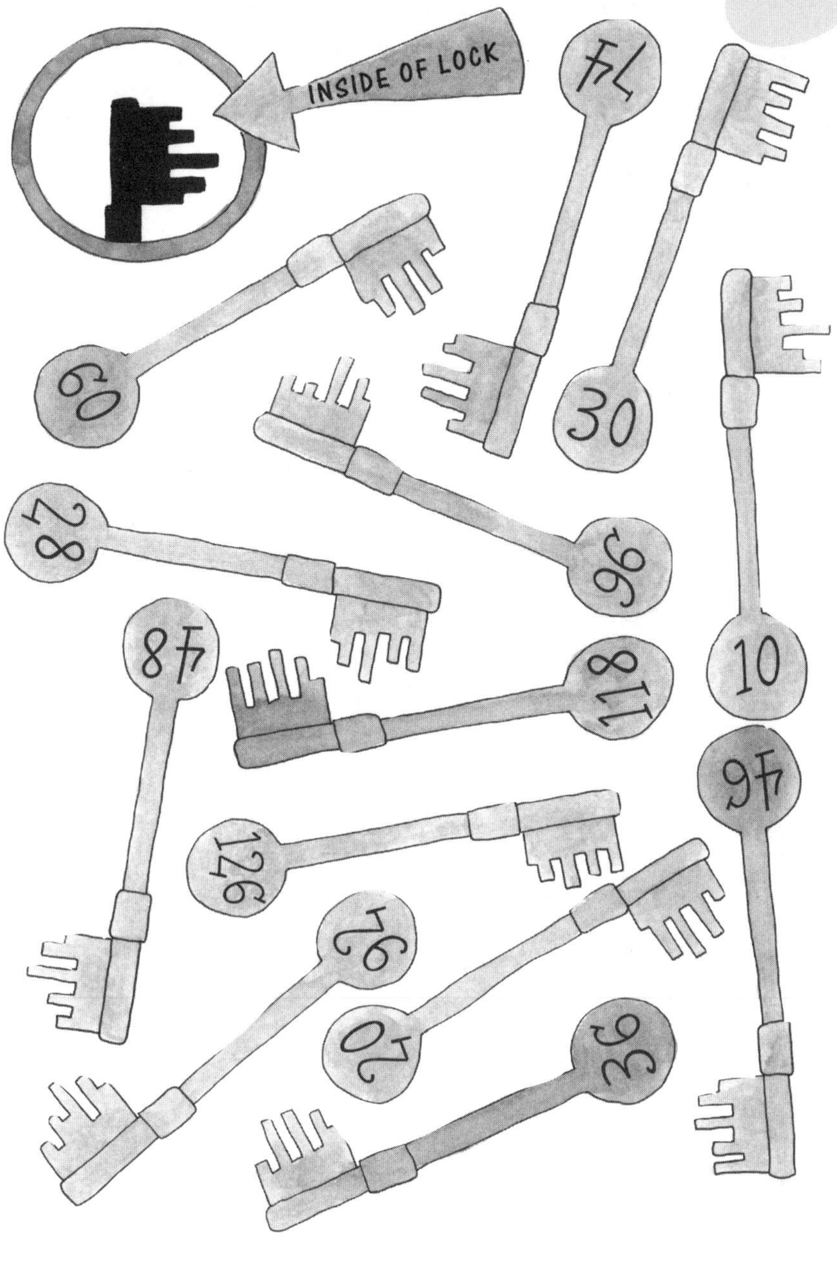
INSIDE OF LOCK
74
60
30
96
28
10
48
118
46
126
92
20
36

Seventy pounds is the correct answer.

'Now if you will excuse me,' said Aunt Jane standing up from the table, 'I must attend to Tizzy's sore tail.'

Tizzy was one of Aunt Jane's many cats which lounged around the house while she fussed over them. As Aunt Jane pottered out into the back garden, she told the children that they were welcome to stay awhile if they could entertain themselves. Lisa scratched her head.

'Whoever is doing all this robbing must be pretty rich by now,' she remarked.

'Yeah,' agreed Sam, but his thoughts were elsewhere.

'The thief must be one of the richest people around,' said Lisa.

'Yeah,' repeated Sam.

'If we could find out who the richest people in Lowtown are, then our thief would probably be among them,' exclaimed Lisa.

'That's it!' shouted Sam, grabbing the rucksack. 'Using Mum's new computer we can access the files from the local bank.'

They found Aunt Jane outside, tying a white bandage around a cat's tail. It looked comical but the children held their laughter. Instead they said goodbye and left.

They rushed back on their bikes to Sam's house. His mum was out so the computer was all theirs. Sam began switching on the computer then he stopped and looked at Lisa with a rather frustrated face.

'I've forgotten that stupid pass number again,' he moaned.

'But I haven't,' said Lisa.

What is the pass number for the computer? (You may need to go back to page 64 if you have forgotten.)
Turn to the same page as your answer.

72

Person number seventy-two is the correct answer.

Almost as soon as they spotted their suspect, he started to move.

'He's getting away!' shouted Sam, throwing his bike against a wall.

Sam and Lisa pushed their way through the crowd keeping their eyes glued to Mr Jones. Every now and then he looked behind him as if to check if he was being followed. Little did he know that he was being stalked by two children.

'Try not to look suspicious,' said Sam, 'and if he sees you, don't make eye contact with him.'

'Easier said than done!' replied Lisa.

Mr Jones crossed the road and headed for the bus stop. He stopped at bus stop number 7 and joined the queue. Sam and Lisa waited until some other people stood behind him and then they too joined the queue, maintaining a safe distance behind their target. Soon a bus pulled up and they all got on. The children sat two seats behind Mr Jones. Sam opened up an abandoned newspaper, ready to use it for cover if Mr Jones turned around. Luckily he didn't.

'He hasn't suspected anything,' whispered Lisa.

'And let's keep it that way,' winked Sam.

Mr Jones changed buses many times. Each time Sam and Lisa followed him. This is the route they took:

As the bus headed for Pink Orchards they got off at bus stop number 11. They took a number 27 bus towards the fruit market and got off at the second stop. Then they took a bus towards Poodle Place via Keyton. They got off at the third stop and took a bus towards Lowtown Centre. They then changed to bus number 36 and got off at the second stop.

What number bus stop did they arrive at?
Turn to the same page as your answer.

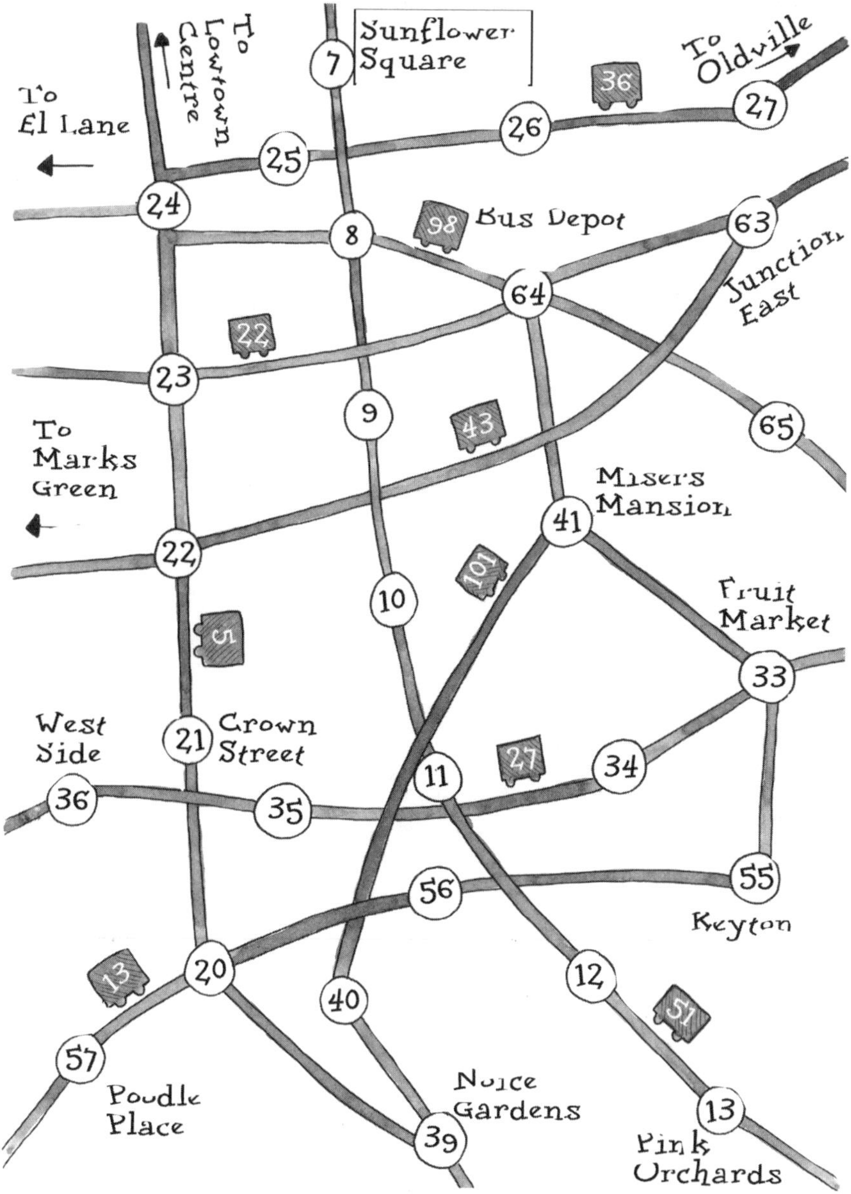
To Lowtown Centre
Sunflower Square
To Oldville
To El Lane
Bus Depot
Junction East
To Marks Green
Misers Mansion
Fruit Market
West Side
Crown Street
Keyton
Noice Gardens
Poodle Place
Pink Orchards
7
24
25
26
27
36
8
98
63
64
22
23
9
43
65
41
22
101
10
5
33
21
34
27
11
36
35
56
55
20
13
40
12
57
51
39
13

The sun is the correct answer to the riddle.

SAM AND LISA ENCOUNTERED ANOTHER MESSAGE AT THE NEXT JUNCTION

?

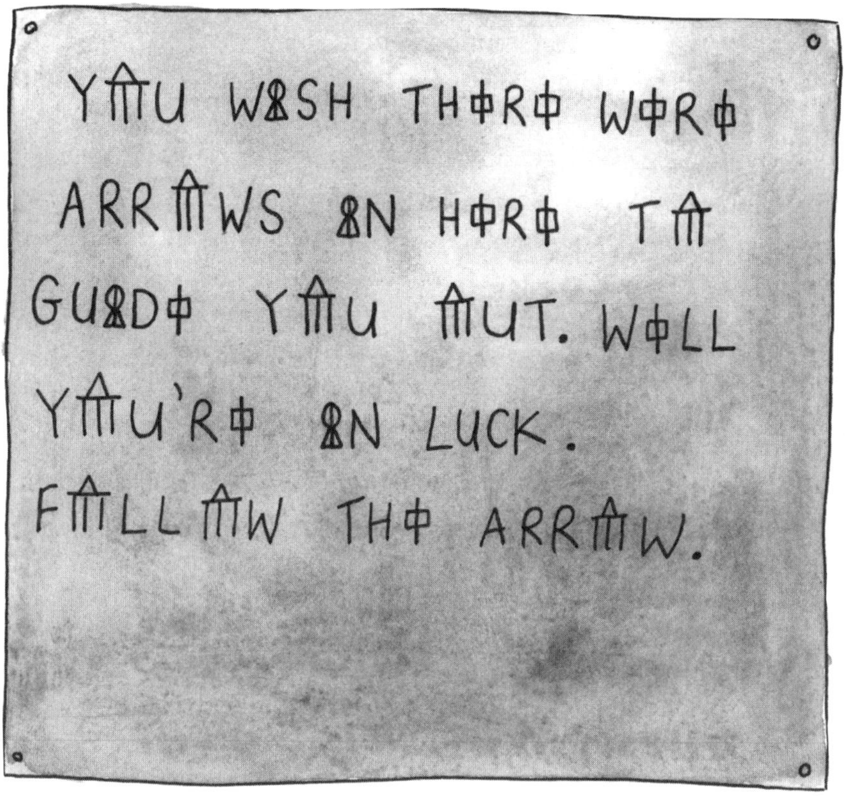

Book number seventy-six is the correct answer.

Sam pulled out the book entitled *C. Kret N Trance*. It had only come part of the way out when he heard a clicking sound and, all of a sudden, the bookshelf started revolving. As it revolved, it opened a gap in the wall.

'Bingo!' shouted Lisa, running through. Sam followed.

The bookshelf continued revolving until it had done a full revolution and once again, the doorway was blocked. Sam and Lisa were now trapped in a narrow room filled with a tangle of cables. Four metal boxes were mounted on the walls. Two on their left and two on their right. A cable led from each box somewhere into the pile of cable on the floor. A flashing red light and the unmistakable word 'ALARM' was on each box. On the wall in front of the children was a heavy duty steel door. A cable from the lock added to the jumble on the floor. On the wall beside the door were five levers. Each lever had a shape above it and a cable running from it to the floor also.

'It looks like one lever opens the door and the other four set off the alarm,' remarked Sam.

'Marvellous!' sighed Lisa.

Which lever opens the door?
Turn to the same page as the symbol on that lever.

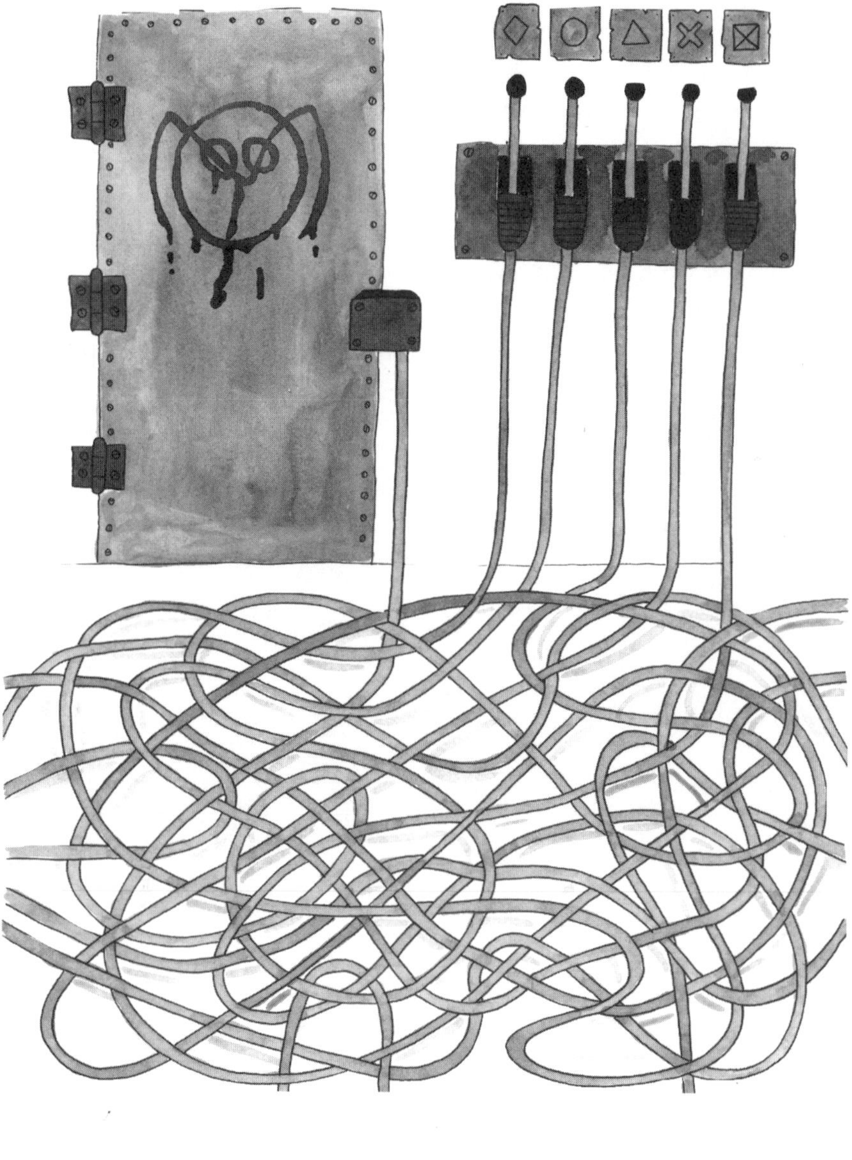

'The mystery is slowly revealing itself,' said Lisa to Sam.

'What?' asked Sam with a frown.

'Never mind,' she said. 'We need to find Mr Jones' office.'

'Why?'

'We need evidence,' explained Lisa, 'because as it is, all we have is what we've seen. That's hardly enough to convict anyone.'

'OK,' agreed Sam, 'but how will we ever find Mr Jones' office? It's hardly going to be signposted.'

'The exact directions are here. I wrote them down when we overheard Salca asking someone in the furnace to show him the way,' grinned Lisa, looking at her notepad. 'Mr Jones' office is north of the games room and south of the bank. It's beside the shop but not beside the bar.'

'OK, what are we waiting for?' said Sam.

Each building has a number.
Which number building is Mr Jones' office in?
Turn to the same page as your answer.

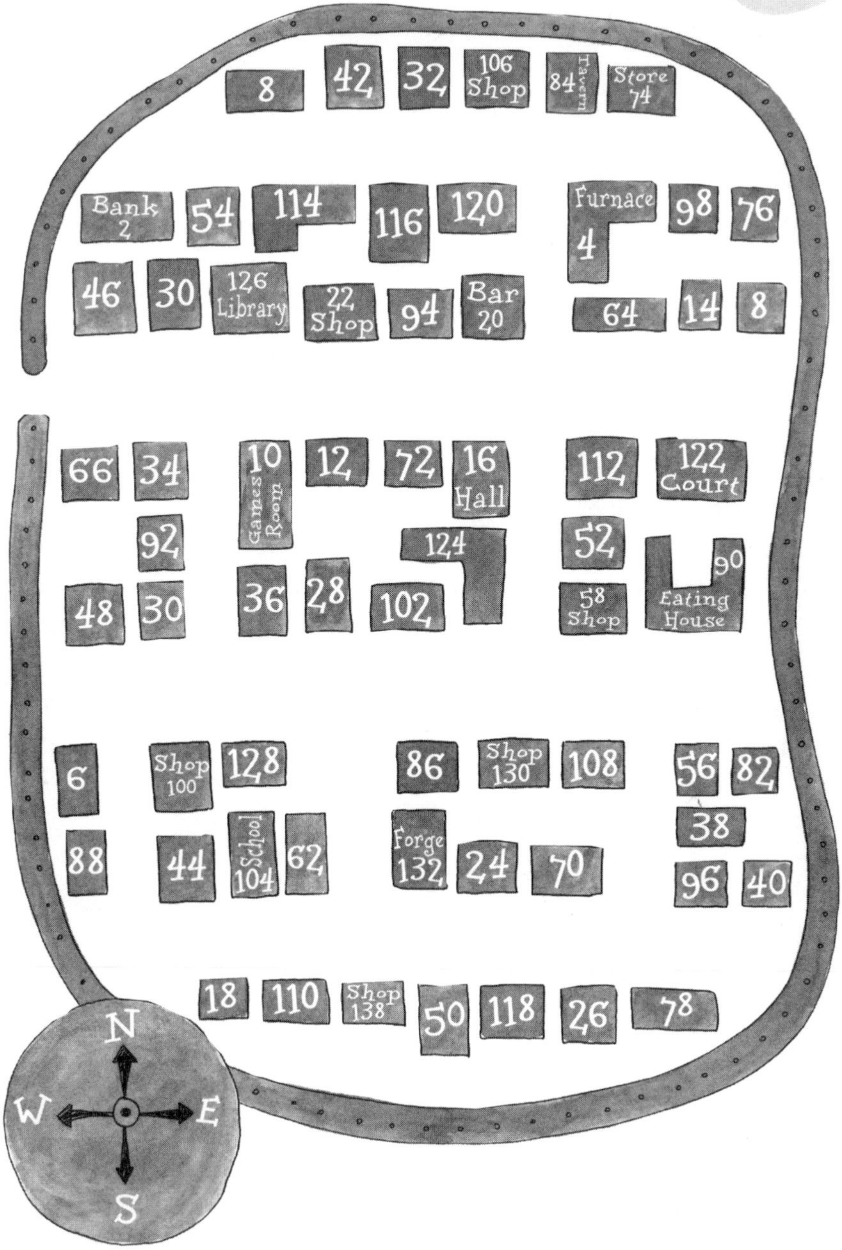
8
42
32
106 Shop
84 Tavern
Store 74
Bank 2
54
114
116
120
Furnace 4
98
76
46
30
126 Library
22 Shop
94
Bar 20
64
14
8
66
34
10 Games Room
12
72
16 Hall
112
122 Court
92
124
52
90 Eating House
48
30
36
28
102
58 Shop
6
Shop 100
128
86
Shop 130
108
56
82
38
88
44
School 104
62
Forge 132
24
70
96
40
18
110
Shop 138
50
118
26
78
N
W
E
S

Exit number eighty is the correct answer.

A short walk through a dark tunnel led them to an enormous underground cavern.

'Wow,' whispered Lisa. 'This place is massive!'

'You could fit all of Lowtown in here,' said Sam.

The cavern was far bigger than any of the other caves they had seen. In the middle of the cavern was what looked like a village. It was surrounded by a stone wall with metal spikes on top. The tops of the houses could be seen over the wall.

'This must be the elf village,' said Sam.

'And it looks like that is the only way in,' said Lisa pointing to the entrance to the village.

The entrance was, however, guarded by an elf-guard who walked back and forth across the entrance. The guard looked nasty and had a scar on one cheek. He wore a helmet and body armour and carried a shield and a long pike. Sam and Lisa waited and waited. Eventually the guard disappeared. Lisa checked her watch. It was 4.58 and 53 seconds. At 4.59 and 23 seconds, a new guard appeared to take up duty.

For how many seconds was the entrance unguarded?
Turn to the same page as your answer.

Key number eighty-two is in the shed.

They found the key and opened the trapdoor to reveal a row of stone steps leading down into the darkness. Sam opened his rucksack.

'One torch for you,' he said, handing Lisa a torch, 'and one for me.'

'I'm not going down there!' muttered Lisa.

'Look, just put one hand on the wall,' said Sam, 'and take one step at a time. Count them as you go. That's what I always do because I don't like heights either.'

Sam switched on his torch and slowly began to descend the steps, counting as he went. Lisa followed, using the same technique.

'One, two, three, four, five,' she counted to herself.

When she got to forty-three, she stopped. She was surrounded by darkness and she was scared. Sam, on the other hand, had reached the bottom of the steps and was waiting patiently for Lisa. He could see her torch light.

'Sam!' she called down to him. 'How many more steps are there?'

'How many have you counted?' shouted Sam.

'Forty-three!' was the reply that he got.

In total, Sam had counted one hundred and five. He called up to her with the answer.

How many more steps has Lisa to go?
Turn to the same page as your answer.

The star is the correct answer to the riddle.

Eventually they reached the end of the maze.

'I don't ever want to see another mixed-up message again,' said Lisa. 'That was hard work.'

'Yeah! My brain is exhausted,' sighed Sam.

The children were now standing in a large cave with a high ceiling. When they spoke, their voices echoed off the walls. The floor was dusty and dotted with pebbles. There were traces of footprints on the floor. Sam found a familiar looking footprint. It had a star shape in the heel.

There were many exits from the cave. Each exit was numbered. Darkness seemed to be the only thing at the other side of the exits although Lisa could have sworn she saw a movement in one of them. When she looked more closely however, she saw nothing. In the middle of the cave on the floor, was a large metal X. It was bolted to the floor.

'Show me that map,' said Lisa. 'This is the place Mammy Long Legs told us about.'

The children examined the map.

'If we follow the instructions on this map,' said Lisa, 'we should be able to find the elf village.'

Which number exit should Sam and Lisa take?

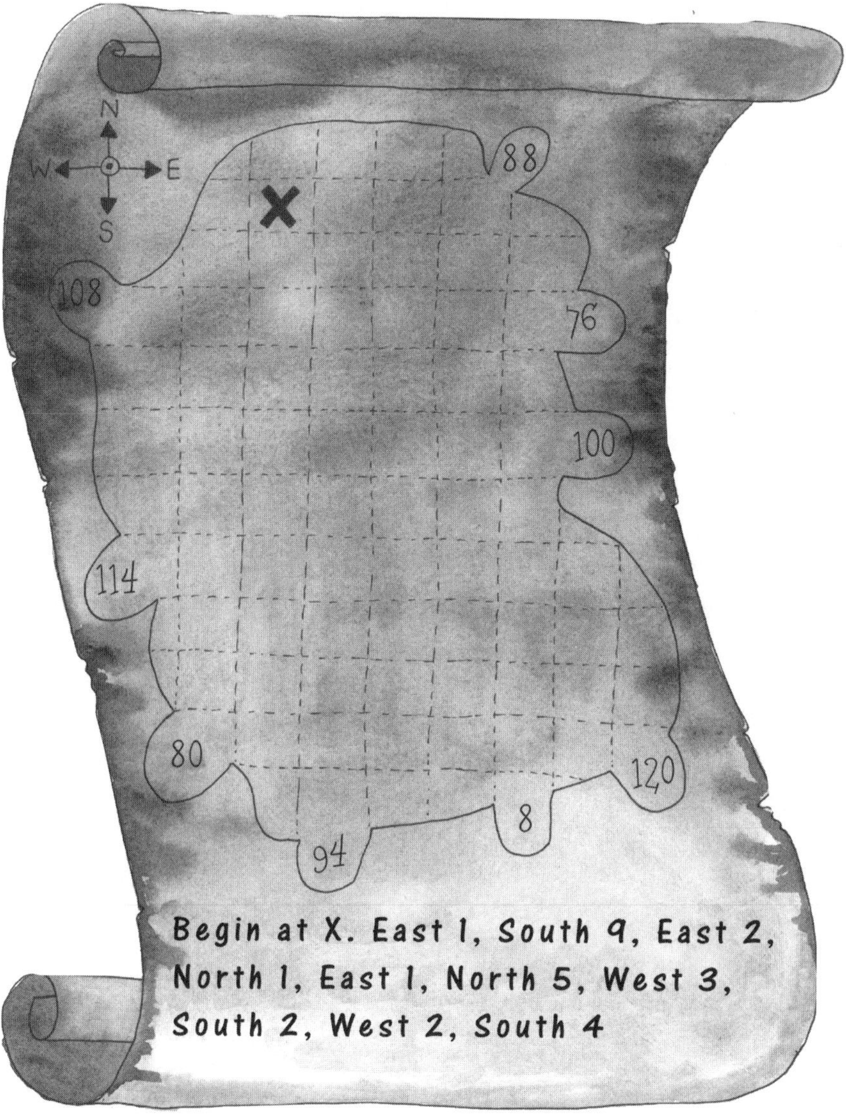
N
W
E
S
X
88
108
76
100
114
80
120
8
94
Begin at X. East 1, South 9, East 2, North 1, East 1, North 5, West 3, South 2, West 2, South 4

The next morning back in Sam's house, the young detectives were no wiser as to who the thief was. Sam was pacing up and down the floor talking to himself.

'Mr Jones has a swanky house. He's obviously loaded – and all those books he has about money!'

'Except for that one called *The Truth about Elves*,' interrupted Lisa.

'Hmm, yes,' said Sam thoughtfully. 'Then there's Mrs Brown. Did you spot the washing on the line, the milk bottles—?'

'And the smoke coming from the chimney,' Lisa joined in. 'But just because Mrs Brown's house is a dump doesn't mean that she's poor. Perhaps she hides the stolen goods under the floorboards knowing that the police wouldn't search a place like hers.'

'There was definitely something suspicious about Mr Johnson. He told me he had fourteen houses but then said he was off to buy his twelfth – unless he can't count! And what could Mr Thompson have so precious that he needs a guard dog?'

These were questions Lisa couldn't answer. Indeed she didn't even try to. She was looking through her photos. She noticed that in each house there were a number of lamps.

'Hey, Sam, do any of these lamps look like your Aunt Jane's?' she asked, spreading the photos out on the table.

'I can't remember what her stupid lamp looks like,' snapped Sam.

'You're useless,' replied Lisa. 'Now let me think. She said it had a square base, a striped lampshade and was dotted with circular, triangular and square stones. It must be one of these.'

Which photo is Aunt Jane's lamp in?
Turn to the same page as the number on that photo.

Photo 72
Photo 24
Photo 26
Photo 68
Photo 18
Photo 42
Photo 84
Photo 44

Lisa looked in through the window of the shop. There was nobody inside. She pushed open the door. A little bell above the door tinkled but still no shopkeeper emerged. Sam followed her in. The shop was narrow but full of goods. The four walls were covered with shelves containing various items, mainly food. Some were recognisable such as fruit and vegetables but there were strange looking tins and bottles with labels such as 'Snaeb' and 'Reeb' and 'Nomel' on them. There was a low counter and a door that led out to the back but still there was no sign of the owner. All of a sudden, the bell tinkled and the shop door opened. Sam and Lisa had their backs to the door. They froze on the spot. They were caught. There was no escape.

'Is there anybody working here?' squeaked a voice behind them. The children turned around to find an elf with a shopping bag in one hand and a white stick in the other. It wore a pair of dark glasses.

Maybe we're not caught after all, thought Lisa to herself. This elf is obviously blind. The children stood out of the way as the elf made its way to the counter.

'How may I help you?' said Sam.

Lisa frowned at him but Sam thought it would be best to serve the customer and then escape without causing suspicion.

'How many bottles of Reeb will I get for these 36 mushrooms?' said the elf putting the bag on the counter.

Sam looked at the chart on the wall.

How many bottles of Reeb will Sam give to the elf?
Turn to the same page as your answer.

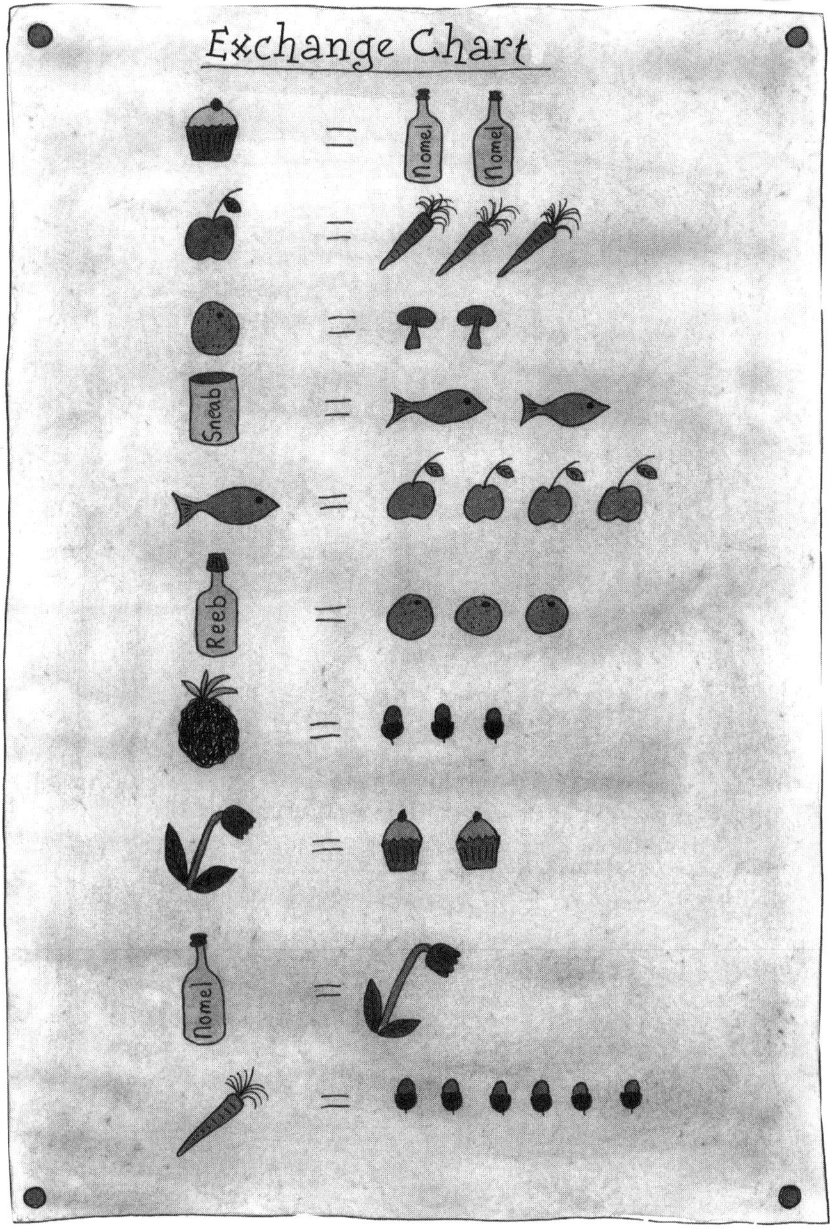
Exchange Chart
Nomel
Nomel
Sneab
Reeb
Nomel

The skull is the correct answer.

Sam and Lisa were about to step onto the bridge, when suddenly a strange creature jumped up from underneath. It was covered all over in hair and had two horns on its head. Its arms were the length of its body and each arm ended with a scaly hand with long dirty fingernails. Its feet were similar. In one of its hands it held a wooden bowl. Two black beady eyes stared at the children from a grinning face.

'A gobbledegook!' whispered Sam to Lisa.

The children were more surprised than scared. After what they had encountered earlier, they believed that nothing could scare them.

'Toll, pweeze,' grunted the gobbledegook, holding out its wooden bowl. A bristly tongue licked its hairy lips.

'We have no money,' said Lisa.

'Hey! Hey! Hey!' laughed the gobbledegook, 'I beweeve you haf twenty-four go coins in you wucksack. Coz am a fay cweature I dont want all you gold. Jus give me one third of da coins . . . Pweeze!

The creature smiled, revealing a set of sharp yellow teeth. Another gobbledegook appeared behind the children. They decided that it would be best to pay. Sam rummaged in the rucksack and pulled out the bag of coins. The creature obviously knew that the bag contained twenty-four coins but perhaps knew nothing about the different values of the different coins. By using the small coins (the halves and quarters) Sam could give the creature one third of the coins without giving away much gold at all.

How many coins should they give the gobbledegook?
Turn to the same page as your answer.

Person number ninety-two is the correct answer.

'It's too late!' cried Sam. 'He's getting away!'

The children watched in despair as Mr Jones got onto a bus which then drove off.

'To think,' said Sam, 'we come this far and then we lose him.'

He looked devastated. Lisa put her arm around him.

'Don't worry,' she said, 'we don't need him any more.'

'What do you mean, we don't need him any more?' frowned Sam.

Lisa pulled out the tape recorder and the sewer map.

'We have all the evidence we need,' she said, 'plus we know that your Aunt Jane's lamp is in Mr Jones' sitting room and we know where tonight's robberies will occur.'

'I suppose you're right,' said Sam. 'But what will we do now?'

'Police station?' suggested Lisa. Sam agreed.

The quickest way to the police station was by bus, but which bus?

Which bus takes the shortest route to the police station? Turn to the same page as the number on that bus.

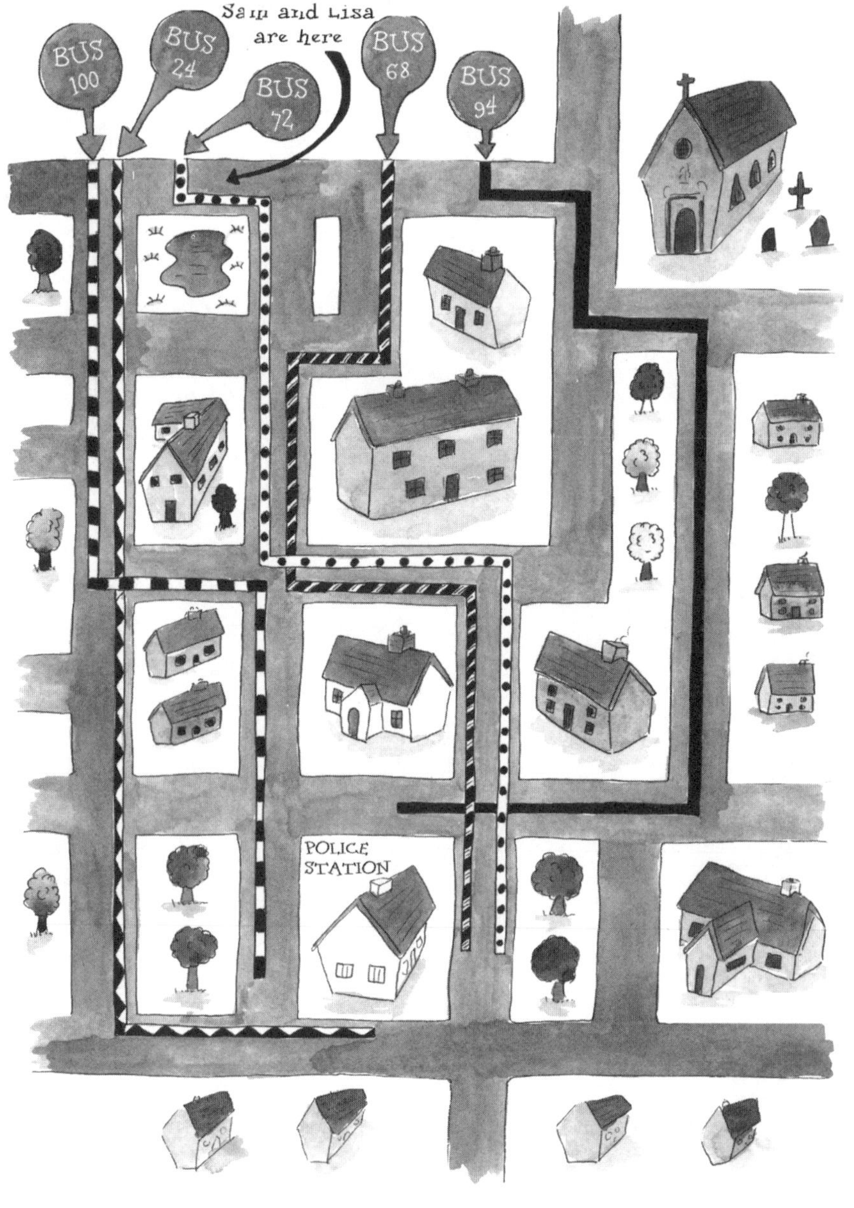
Sam and Lisa are here
BUS 100
BUS 24
BUS 72
BUS 68
BUS 94
POLICE STATION

The arrow is the correct answer to the riddle.

ANOTHER MESSAGE IN CODE TOLD SAM AND LISA WHICH WAY TO GO

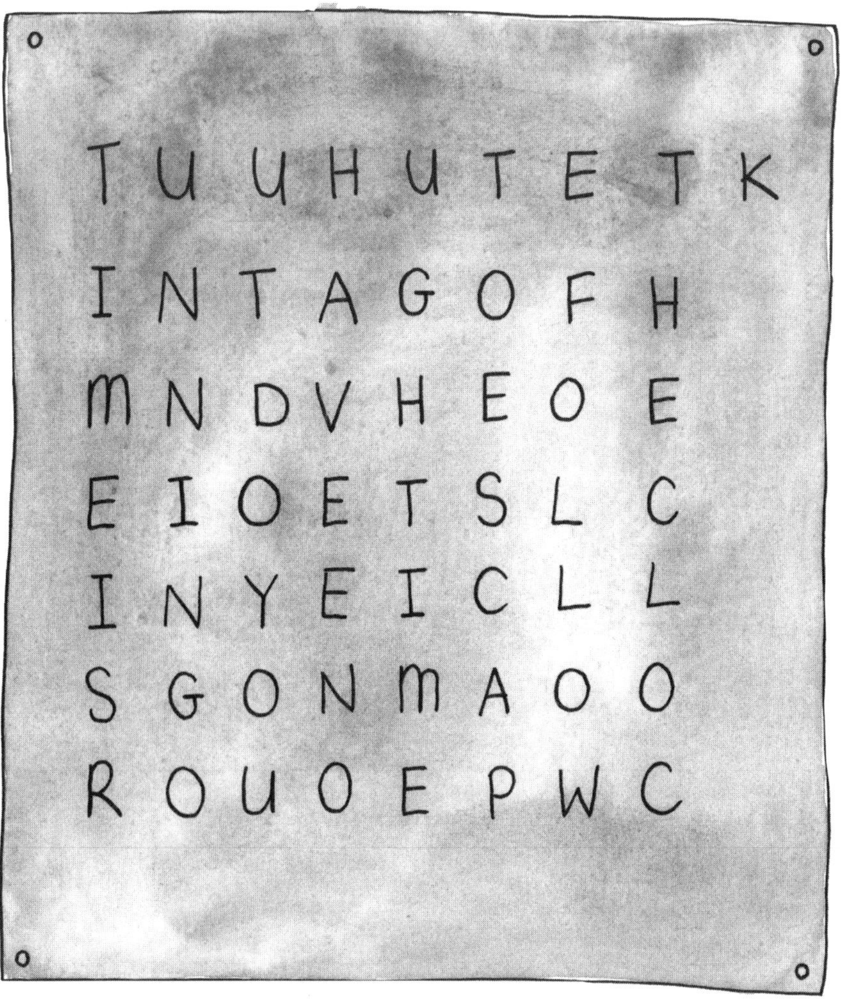
T U U H U T E T K
I N T A G O F H
M N D V H E O E
E I O E T S L C
I N Y E I C L L
S G O N M A O O
R O U O E P W C

D 96

Ninety-six boxes of gold is the correct answer.

Suddenly the door of the store room opened. Sam and Lisa ducked behind a pile of boxes. A little elf stumbled into the room carrying a box of gold. He placed it on the ground and then from the box he took out a piece of paper. It was another graph. He stuck it on the wall and took down the old graph, which he carefully folded up and put in his pocket. With a pencil he marked the new graph and then left the room. Sam and Lisa looked at each other in horror as they heard the door being locked. Lisa raced over to the door. Her worst fears were confirmed. It was locked.

Sam looked through the keyhole.

'The key is still in the door,' he said optimistically.

'Yeah, and that's a lot of good to us,' cried Lisa.

Sam wasn't listening to her. He had already taken down the new graph from the wall and slipped it under the locked door, being careful to leave one edge of the paper inside the room.

'What are you doing?' asked Lisa.

Sam didn't answer. He was concentrating on his notepad which was in his hand. The notepad was bound together by a spiral wire. Sam pulled the wire out and straightened it in his hands. He then stuck one end of the wire into the keyhole and began moving it about. Lisa smiled when she realised what he was doing. A few minutes later, the sound of the key dropping to the ground could be heard. It landed on the piece of paper at the other side of the door. Sam pulled the piece of paper back under the door and with it came the key.

'Who said television isn't educational?' said Sam, opening the door.

The children sneaked out, after having put everything back the way it had been.

Turn back to page 30.

STORE

Mr Jones, 98 Old Street.

Mr Jones' house was one in a row of red-bricked houses. It was surrounded by a brick wall. A pretty little garden lay at the front of the house. As they approached, the children could see the top of a garden shed at the back. They parked their bikes at the front gate.

It's a neat house, thought Sam looking at the window boxes full of colourful flowers. Lisa plucked up the courage to ring the door bell. There was no answer. Sam looked in through one of the lower front windows of the house.

'Come here!' he shouted. Lisa ran over. 'Look at all the books this guy's got.'

Lisa peered in through the pane of glass. She saw a tall wooden bookcase. It was crammed with books of different sizes and shapes.

'He must have a boring life,' said Sam. 'All the books are about the same thing.'

'Not them all,' replied Lisa. 'I can see one book which looks odd among the others.'

What is the odd book that Lisa has spotted?
Turn back to page 34.

The Dollar Scholar
All About The Money
PENNIES AND POUNDS
Value for your Pound
What to do with your money
FLASH THE CASH
HOW TO SAVE MONEY
Buying and Selling
Spending and Saving
Get more from your money
101 things to do with money
Money in your MATTRESS
BECOME RICH IN A MONTH
From Rags to Riches
The Rich and the Poor
Every Penny Counts
The Money Market
POUNDS, PENCE & PESETAS
WHAT TO DO WITH YOUR MONEY
A Bank Balancing Act
MONEY, MONEY, MONEY
At the End of the Rainbow
Pennies From Heaven
WEALTH
The World's Wealthiest People
A Hole in the Wallet
Spon Doola's Bank '92-'93
Pennies for them
LOOSENED PURSE STRINGS
Money Makes the World Go Round
ROB THE POOR TO HELP THE RICH
1000 Richest People
Money Matters or does it?
Pennies upon Pennies
FUNNY MONEY
Making Cash go Further
BUYING MONEY
THE RICH AND THE RICHER
In for a Penny
Pots of Dosh
Bank On It!
MONEY!!!
Become a Millionaire in Minutes
WHAT ARE YOU WORTH?
The Truth about Elves
Business Directory 2000
Plastic Money
MAKE MONEY FAST
CASH BACK!
The Millionaire with No Bank Account
THE BANK
LOLLY!
A SHARE OF THE WEALTH
HOBBIES: COUNTING MONEY
Safes, Locks and Securities
The Collapse of the River Bank

Bus number one hundred is the correct answer.

Sam and Lisa told their story to the police. Having seen and heard their evidence, the police were still not convinced. Who would believe that a gang of little elves had been climbing out of toilets in Lowtown's houses, stealing all around them and then escaping back down without even using the flush? Eventually Sam and Lisa persuaded the police to stake out a bathroom on Smellington Street that night.

In the middle of the night, as the children had predicted, a little elf's head peeped up over the toilet seat. At the sight of two policemen staring at him with their mouths open, the elf returned the way he had come, very quickly.

The next day Mr Jones was brought in for questioning. Sam and Lisa were later invited down to the police station for an identity parade.

'We nearly have enough proof to send this thief to jail,' said the sergeant. 'There's just one more thing we need,' he said. 'If you can identify Mr Jones from these four men, then we'll probably be presenting him with a bread and water dinner menu every day for the next fifteen years.'

'No problem,' chorused the two friends.

'I'd know him anywhere,' said Sam confidently.

'Yeah, me too,' smiled Lisa. 'After all, we did spend long enough watching him.'

Which man is Mr Jones? (To refresh your memory of him, turn to page 39.)
Turn to the same page as his symbol.

A
B
C
D

102

The candle is the correct answer to the riddle.

THE NEXT JUNCTION IN THE MAZE CONTAINED A SIMILAR MESSAGE FOR SAM AND LISA

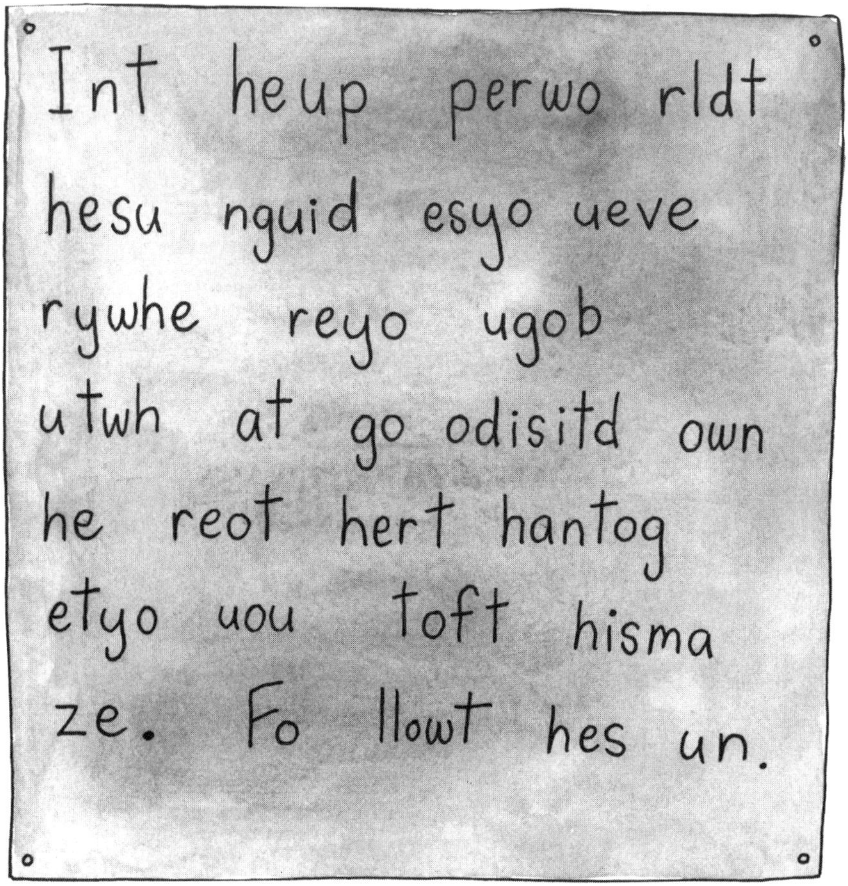
Int heup perwo rldt
hesu nguid esyo ueve
rywhe reyo ugob
utwh at go odisitd own
he reot hert hantog
etyo uou toft hisma
ze. Fo llowt hes un.

The flower is the symbol on the torn note.

Swiftly they climbed out of Mr Jones' house, back over the side gate and grabbed their bikes.

'Wait,' said Lisa, just as they were about to leave. 'Even if we do get there by 12.00, how will we know who this Mr Jones is? That square is always crowded and we don't even know what he looks like.'

'You're right,' said Sam.

He looked around. Mr Jones' neighbour, an old woman, was cutting the grass in her front lawn. Sam wheeled his bike over to her house.

'Excuse me,' he said. The woman stopped her mowing. 'We were speaking to Mr Jones on the telephone last night,' said Sam, 'and we arranged to meet him in Sunflower Square at twelve o'clock to do an interview with him for the school newspaper. We have just realised that we don't know what he looks like. We were wondering if you could help us.'

'Sure,' said the old woman. 'He's about average height, bald, wears glasses, shirt and tie and often carries a briefcase.'

'Thanks,' said Sam.

'It's now 11.22,' said Lisa looking at her watch. 'We'd better hurry!'

How many minutes have they got to get to Sunflower Square?
Turn to the same page as your answer.

Number one hundred and six is the correct answer.

'Judging by the speed with which you entered I can only presume that the elf-guards were chasing you,' said Mammy Long Legs. Sam and Lisa nodded in agreement. 'Well, don't worry,' she assured them, 'you're safe. They won't come up here. They know better than that. Anyway, I'm surprised the gobbledegooks didn't get you or did you "pweese" them in some way?'

'With gold coins,' answered Sam.

'That'd be right!' she snapped. 'A few gold pieces will keep those ignorant savages happy for weeks. They spend their whole lives collecting gold and other valuables which are actually worthless to them because they can't spend any of it. Now that I've saved your skins, you can entertain me for a while. If you impress me, then I will help you, but if you don't, well, then it's back down that ladder.'

Mammy Long Legs reached behind her and produced a pack of playing cards.

'I have removed the twelve coloured cards so that we are left with forty numbered cards. We're now going to play a game called 'forty card pick up'. Are you familiar with that game?' asked Mammy Long Legs looking at her guests.

The children shook their heads.

'You'll catch on quick enough,' smiled Mammy Long Legs.

She began dealing out the cards so quickly that you could hardly see her hands. After a few seconds the cards were dealt onto the floor, face up, in front of Sam and Lisa.

'Now pick them up, in order,' said Mammy Long Legs, 'and check if there are any cards missing. I think there is one.'

The children set to work.

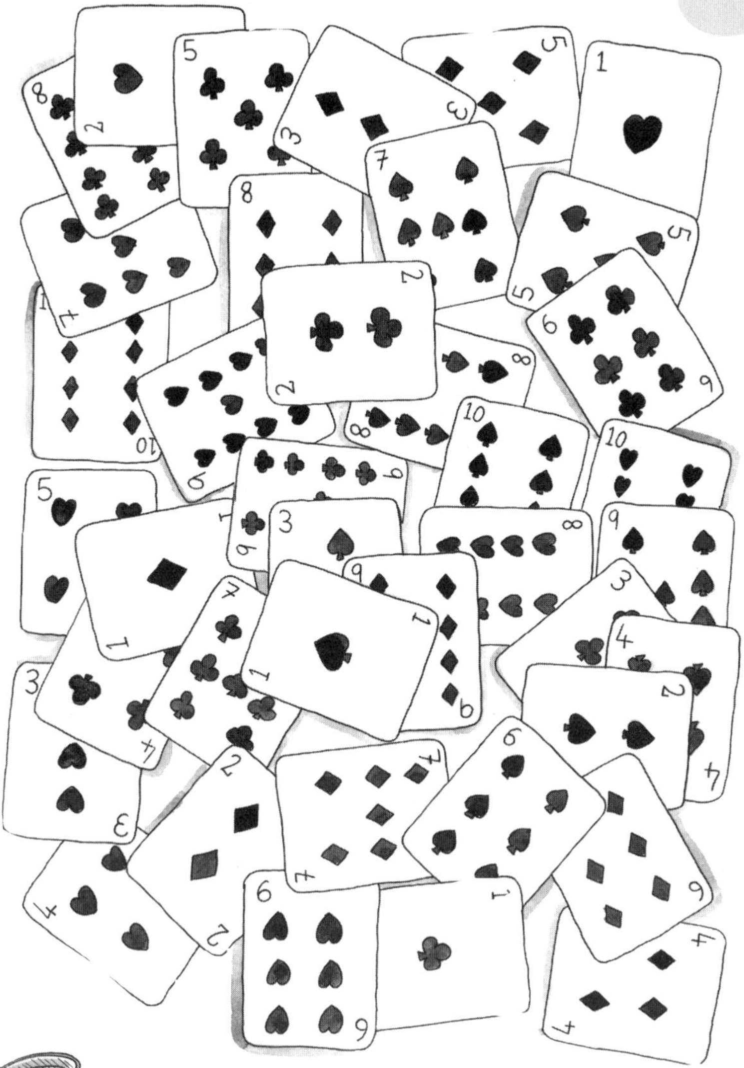

There are only 39 cards in the picture.
One card is missing.
What is the missing card?
Turn to the same page as the number on that card.

One of the windows of the furnace building was open. Sam and Lisa looked in. They could feel heat on their faces. Inside many elves were busy at work. At one table, two elves were sorting jewellery into different bundles. Another elf was throwing fuel into a hot furnace in the centre of the floor. Earrings, necklaces, bracelets, rings and other golden objects were being put into a funnel above the furnace. This gold was being melted down and then poured into small circular moulds which entered a machine along a conveyor belt. On the other side of the machine, the gold came out in the form of gold coins. A wooden box was slowly filling up with these gold coins.

The outside door opened and an elf, holding a piece of paper, entered. Everybody stopped working.

'Hello,' said the elf. 'My name is Salca. I'm new here and I've received this message to go to Mr Jones' office. He has given me the instructions about how to get into his office but he didn't tell me where it is. Perhaps someone could show me.'

One of the elves gave Salca directions. Lisa memorised them and then wrote them down in her notepad.

'This elf will lead us straight to Mr Jones,' smiled Sam.

'You're right,' said Lisa, 'so get a good look at him because we may need to follow him from a distance.'

Each elf has a number.
Can you find Salca?
Turn to the same page as the number on Salca.

42
94
68
54
66
28
90
64
32
44
34
52
88
78
56

110

The clock is the correct answer to the riddle.

'NOT ANOTHER STUPID MESSAGE,' SIGHED SAM AT THE SIGHT OF THE NEXT JUNCTION IN THE MAZE.

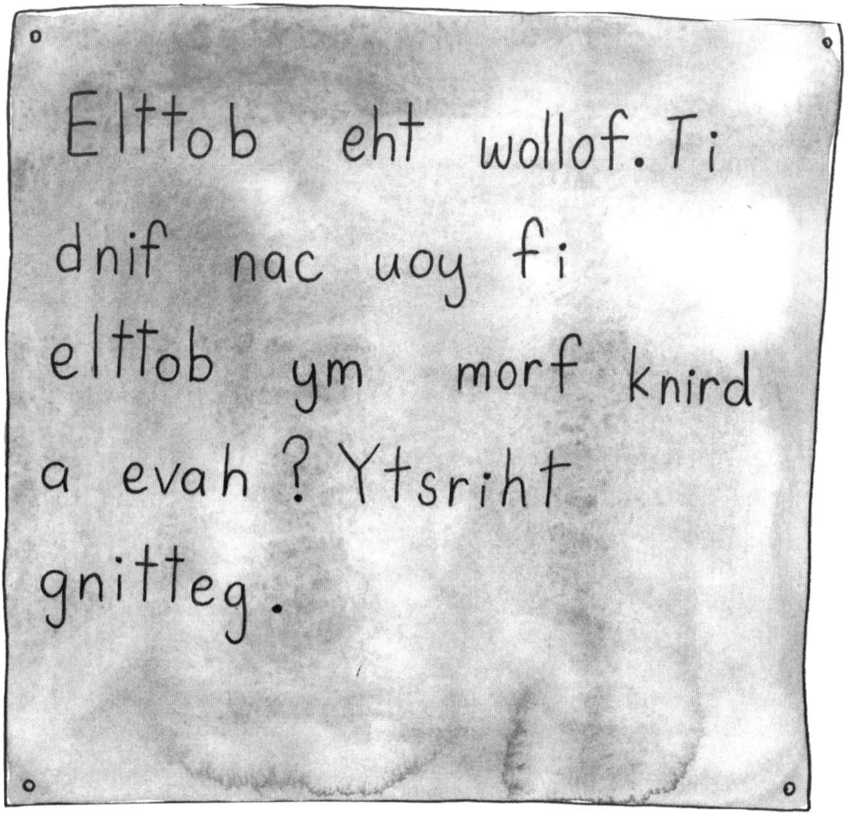
Elttob eht wollof. Ti
dnif nac uoy fi
elttob ym morf knird
a evah? Ytsriht
gnitteg.

The door is the correct answer.

'DOOR! That's it!' cried Lisa.

'Yeah, great!' said Sam. 'But that's only a word. We're still stuck in this old room.'

Lisa thought for a moment and then stood on the letter D. She slowly walked onto O, and then the other O and then R. They heard a click followed by a rumbling noise from the opposite wall. Light flooded through as a secret stone door began to open in the wall. The children stared in amazement at this spectacle. Soon the door was fully open, but then, before their eyes it began to close again.

'Quick! Let's go!' shouted Lisa, grabbing Sam's hand.

They raced through the exit just before the door came to a grinding close behind them. They found themselves in a stone room similar to the last except that it had a large wooden door on one wall. Lisa tried the door.

'It's locked,' she said, looking into the metal keyhole.

In the middle of each of the remaining three walls, there was a metal safe. Each safe was locked with a combination lock. On each safe was what looked like a clue to the combination of the lock.

'Maybe the key for this door is in one of these safes,' suggested Lisa.

They looked at the first safe.

'I remember doing these in school!' she exclaimed. 'All you have to do is work out the pattern that the numbers make.'

Can you work out the missing number in the combination for the lock?
Turn to the same page as your answer.

14, —, 26, 32, 38, 44, 50

The door of the tavern was open so Sam and Lisa sneaked in. They crouched low behind a barrel. The pub was full of elves. A large fat elf stood behind the bar, pouring a purple liquid into small cups. All the elves seemed to be drinking this. Clouds of smoke rose from pipes which the elves were smoking. One group of elves was deep in conversation. They looked nervous and at times their voices became mere whispers. Other less sociable drinkers stood around staring into space. Close to Sam and Lisa, a group of elves was kneeling on the ground playing some kind of dice game.

Suddenly something touched Sam's leg. It was a dice. Then he looked up to find four elves staring over the barrel at him.

'Well, well, well, what have we got here?' said one of the elves.

Lisa was quick with an answer.

'We're doing some observation work for Mr Jones,' she explained.

The elves were silent. Eventually one of them spoke.

'I don't believe you,' he announced.

Another elf ran to the bar and returned with a piece of slate and a stick of chalk.

He handed it to Lisa, saying, 'If you work for Mr Jones, you should know the elf symbol. Draw it for me.'

Lisa took the chalk and started thinking. She knew she had seen the symbol before.

Turn to the page with the elf symbol.

The store room was unguarded. Lisa knocked on the door and then she and Sam hid behind a pile of empty wooden boxes along the wall outside. They waited. There was no answer so the children slowly opened the door, looked all around and then slipped in. The room was full of small wooden boxes, stacked on top of each other. Lisa examined one of them. It was jammed with gold coins.

'Wow!' she gasped lifting up a handful of coins. 'There must be millions of pounds worth of gold in here!'

'Imagine all the things I could buy with even a few coins,' drooled Sam examining the contents of a box. 'New bike, clothes, games, skateboard, computer, television, video, stereo, holiday,' he mumbled to himself.

'Yes, but the money is not yours so forget it!' interrupted Lisa.

'But it doesn't really belong to Mr Jones or any of these elves,' argued Sam.

'That's right,' said Lisa. 'If you take any of this gold, you're taking it from your Aunt Jane and the rest of the residents in Lowtown. Let's not forget that we have a job to do so put the gold back and let's get on with it.'

'I suppose you're right,' sighed Sam flinging the coins back into the box but he smiled to himself as he suddenly remembered the gold coins already in his rucksack!

'Look!' said Lisa, pointing to a piece of paper on the wall. 'It's a graph and it shows how many boxes were put in here last week.'

How many boxes of gold were put into the store room last week?
Turn to the same page as your answer.

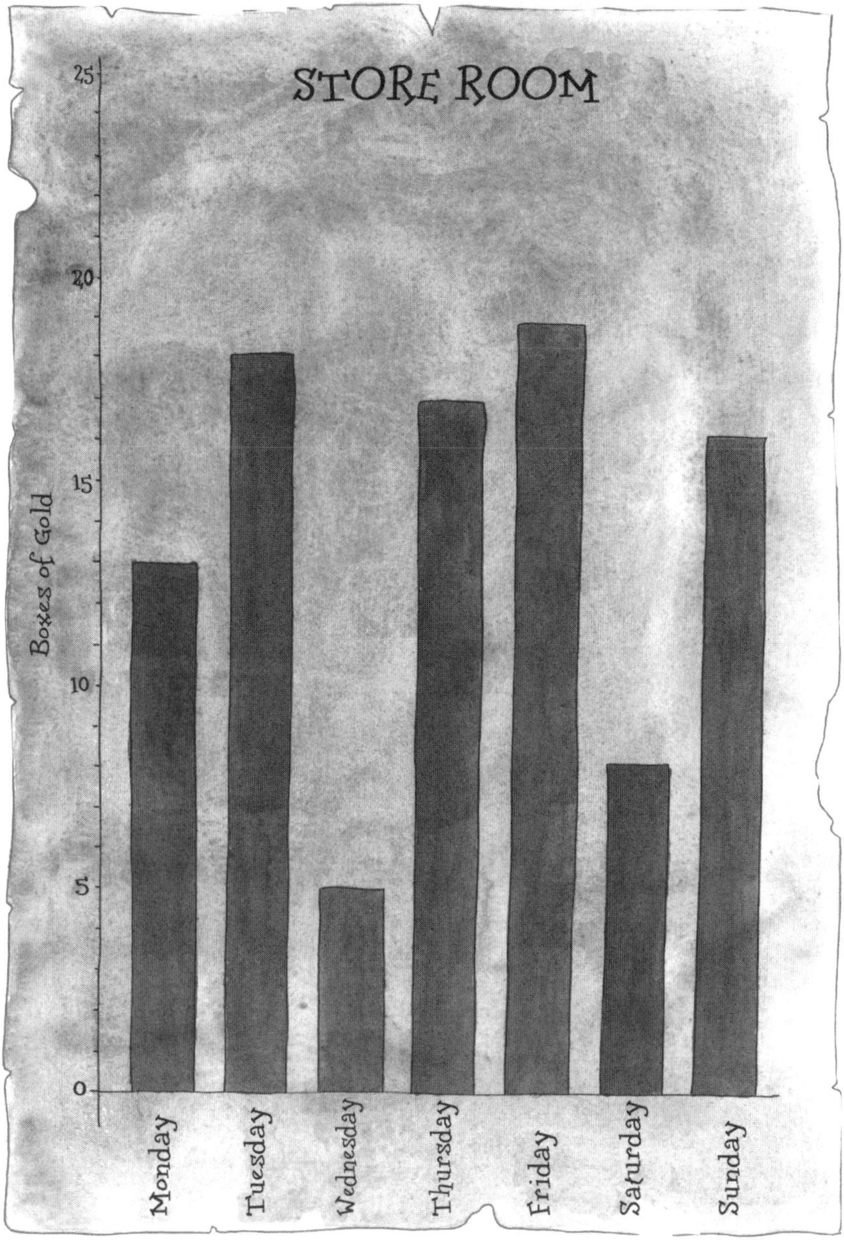
STORE ROOM
Boxes of Gold
25
20
15
10
5
0
Monday
Tuesday
Wednesday
Thursday
Friday
Saturday
Sunday

The spiral is the correct symbol in the picture.

A few minutes walk led Sam and Lisa to the Maze of Mixed-Up Messages. A metal plate on the entrance wall gave them instructions for the maze:

> All the walls in this maze contain symbols. At each junction in the maze there is a riddle telling you to follow a symbol. If you follow the correct symbols you will reach the other side of the maze. If you don't then you may be lost forever.
>
> Sounds easy doesn't it? Well it's not! The riddles at each junction are mixed up (like your brain will be if you get lost in here!).

Boldly, Sam and Lisa entered the maze. As predicted, when they came to the first junction there was a riddle on the wall. A set of mixed-up instructions told them which way to go.

'This looks like your handwriting Sam, it's so difficult to read,' smirked Lisa pointing to the riddle.

Sam laughed. 'Well then, that means that you're going to need me to get out of here,' he replied, 'so you should be nice to me.'

The children looked at the riddle on the wall. This wasn't going to be easy.

Work out the riddle.
Turn to the same page as that symbol.
Do the same at the other junctions in the maze.

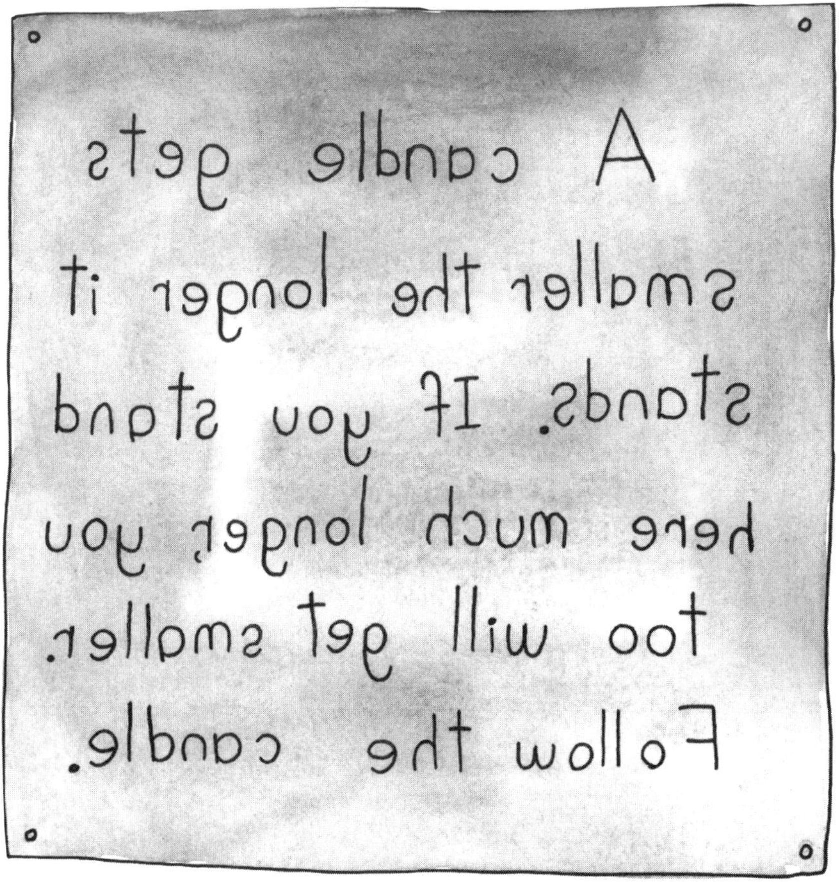
A candle gets smaller the longer it stands. If you stand here much longer you too will get smaller. Follow the candle.

The carrot is the symbol in the picture.

Sam and Lisa sat on top of the trapdoor puffing and panting.

'Welcome!' said a voice.

The children jumped with fright. A strange creature sat on a pile of square tiles in the corner of a room. It had large eyes with long eyelashes and pouting lips. Antennae protruded from its head. These were not the strangest things about this creature. It had four arms and two legs that were so long and skinny, the children wondered why it needed a ladder to enter its home. It wore a yellow bikini top and shorts and had a shoe on one foot. Two transparent wings stuck out of its back.

'Welcome to my home,' the creature said, in a very polite voice. Its home was a large cave but was decorated entirely with things from the human world. Old stuff like statues, lanterns and bowler hats were combined with things like lamps, radios, posters and telephones so that the room looked like a museum dedicated to the history of household goods.

'My name is Mammy Long Legs,' said the creature, 'and I can see by looking at you that you are impressed with my home. Perhaps, seeing as you are now my guests, you would like to make a donation.'

Lisa stuck her head into the rucksack and pulled out Sam's magnifying glass, much to his annoyance. Mammy Long Legs stretched out one of her spindly arms and accepted the gift with pleasure. She hung it up from the ceiling, beside a model aeroplane. Lisa could see that she was delighted with it.

Multiply the number of tiles by the number of legs by the number of arms and add 50.
Turn to the page with that number.

Mrs Brown, 122 Spider Street.

After a short cycle, Sam and Lisa arrived on Spider Street. Mrs Brown's house was old, dirty and very run down. It had a rotten wooden veranda which was littered with pieces of wood, an axe, a wheelbarrow and other bits of junk. Weeds and bushes grew up through gaps in the boards. The windows were either smashed or boarded up while the gutters were rusted and falling down. Bushes, trees and plants grew wild as if trying to strangle the house. A tree, which was now dead, had grown up through the roof. Dust, dirt and cobwebs lay everywhere. Wiping some dust off one of the windows Lisa looked in.

'It's the same inside,' she said to Sam.

She took a photo of the room inside and proceeded around the house to do the same through the other windows. Sam did some investigating of his own.

'Maybe nobody lives here anymore,' said Lisa.

'No,' replied Sam, 'somebody lives here all right.'

There are three clues in the picture to suggest that somebody does live in the house. Can you spot them?
Turn back to page 34.

Number one hundred and twenty-four is the answer.

'Maybe it's dead,' whispered Sam.

A voice moaned from under the hood, 'You're right. I am dead.'

Sam and Lisa screamed, turned on their heels and began running as fast as they could back down the tunnel.

'STOP!' the voice roared. The children froze in their tracks. 'There is no way out, except past me!'

Slowly, Sam and Lisa turned around. The figure was now standing. It was the height of the tunnel.

'I am dead,' it groaned. 'I have no body . . . and no, that does not mean I am lonely. It means I have NO BODY!'

It pulled down its hood to reveal a white skull as a head. Sam and Lisa were terrified. It started to speak again.

'I am the gatekeeper. I guard the entrance to the elf world. I shall ask you a question. Get the answer right and you may enter. Get it wrong and you shall join my collection of bones further up the passage.'

The tall dark figure pulled out a large axe from under its cloak. The children shuddered.

'Think of a number, any number,' said the skeleton, 'now add 11, Take away 4. Add 7. Take away the number you first thought of. What is the answer?'

What is the answer?
Turn to the same page as your answer.

Mr Jones' office is in building number one hundred and twenty-six.

Lisa pushed open the old door of the library. There was nobody inside. In fact, the place looked like it was never even used. Everything was covered in dust, and cobwebs stretched from the ceiling to the floor.

'For a place that's supposed to be a library it doesn't have many books,' said Sam.

There was only one bookcase of dusty books. Apart from an old desk and two chairs, the place was empty. There was no door out of the room except the one that they had just come in through.

'This can't be Mr Jones' office,' said Sam. 'Are you sure we have the right building?'

'Positive,' replied Lisa.

'Maybe there's a hidden door in here somewhere,' said Sam.

'Let's try that bookcase,' urged Lisa.

'Hey look at this book,' exclaimed Sam pulling down a book entitled *Human Children*.

He opened up the book and began reading.

'Lisa, listen to this,' said Sam. 'It says here that "human children are the most annoying members of the human race. They are extremely meddlesome and quite likely to discover entrances to our world. Luckily they are stupid and so their parents never believe the stories they tell of having seen elves. Fortunately, children are not very strong either and do not carry lethal weapons – unlike the grown-ups. When encountering one, an elf should frighten the child severely and return it to the upper world. Normally this will be the end of the matter."'

'We're obviously two exceptions to the rule,' smiled Lisa. 'Now let's try and find that hidden door.'

One of the books opens a hidden door.
Which book is it?
Turn to the same page as the number on that book.

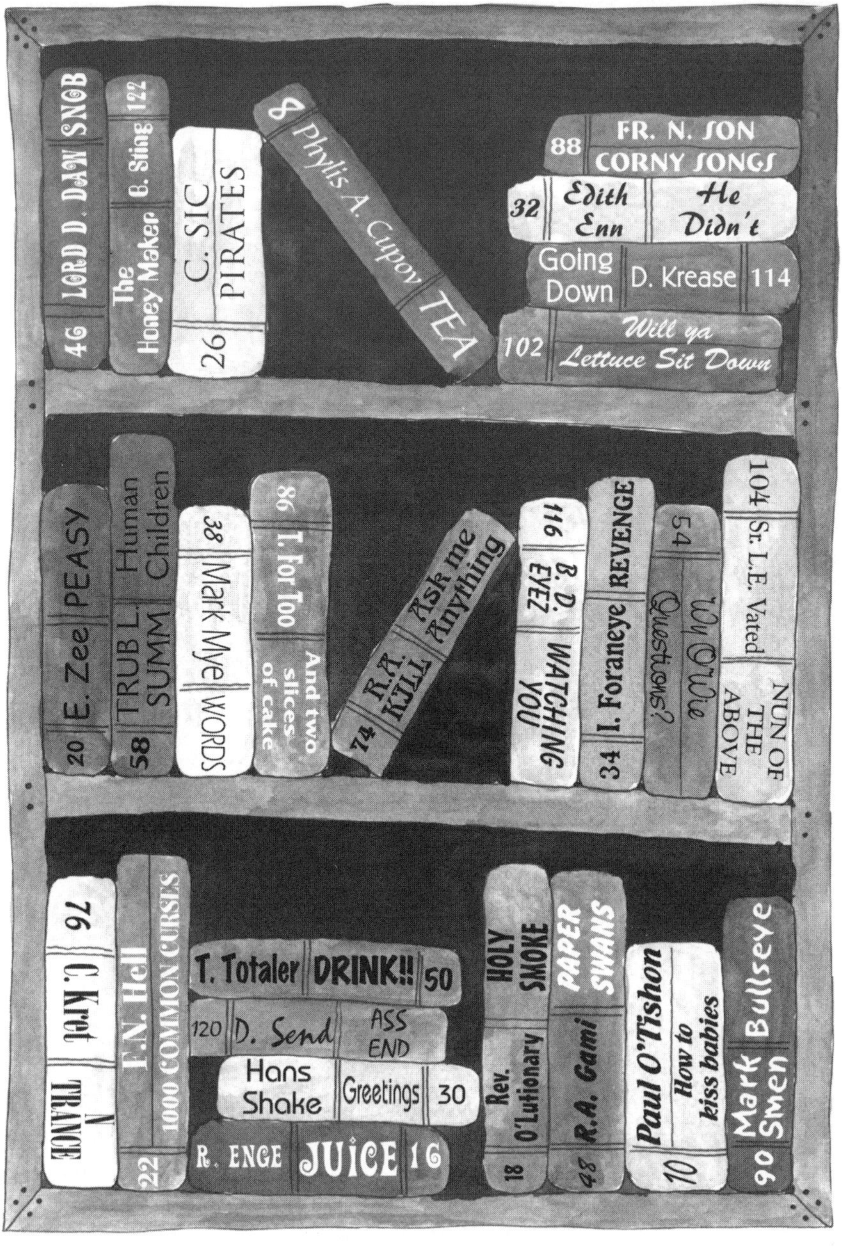
LORD D. DAW SNOB 46
The Honey Maker B. Sting 122
C. SIC PIRATES 26
Phylis A. Cupov TEA 8
FR. N. SON CORNY SONGS 88
Edith Enn He Didn't 32
Going Down D. Krease 114
Will ya Lettuce Sit Down 102
E. Zee PEASY 20
TRUB L. SUMM Human Children 58
Mark Mye WORDS 38
T. For Too And two slices of cake 86
R.A. KILL Ask me Anything 74
B.D. EVEZ WATCHING YOU 116
I. Foraneye REVENGE 34
Wy O'Wie Questions? 54
Sr. L.E. Vated NUN OF THE ABOVE 104
C. Kret N TRANCE 76
F.N. Hell 1000 COMMON CURSES 22
T. Totaler DRINK!! 50
D. Send ASS END 120
Hans Shake Greetings 30
R. ENGE JUICE 16
Rev. O'Lutionary HOLY SMOKE 18
R.A. Gami PAPER SWANS 48
Paul O'Tishon How to kiss babies 10
Mark Smen Bullseye 90

A 128

A is the correct Mr Jones.

Two days later Mr Jones was convicted of grand scale robbery. It turned out that he had accidentally discovered the elf world and then enslaved the vulnerable elves to do his dirty work. Having heard Sam and Lisa's story, it was agreed that the elves and their underground world should remain a secret. Judges, jury, police and anybody else who became involved with the case, had to take a solemn oath never to utter a word to anybody about the elf world. If they did, they would be charged with treason.

And so the elves were left in peace to once again lead their lives as normal. Sam and Lisa were richly rewarded, but to be safe, they never told anybody, even the police, where the entrances to the elf world were. That was the only way they could be sure the secret would remain a secret.

And the next time you sit on a toilet seat, just remember who or what could be lurking beneath you!

The End

Page	Answer	Page	Answer	Page	Answer	Page	Answer
4	64	36	12	70	34	100	128
8	56	38	72	72	26	102	74
10	32	40	22	74	94	104	38
12	92	43	104	76	46	107	10
14	90	44	28	78	126	108	54
16	120	47	52	80	30	110	58
18	44	48	124	82	62	112	20
20	40	52	36	84	80	114	50
22	68	56	16	86	42	116	96
26	82	58	84	88	6	118	102
28	70	62	112	90	8	120	106
30	78	64	18	92	100	124	14
32	66	66	118	94	110	126	76
34	86	68	48				